BETWEEN A ROCK AND A COWBOY

LEXI POST

OLIVERHEBERBOOKS

All rights reserved.

No part of this publication may be sold, copied, distributed, reproduced or transmitted in any form or by any means, mechanical or digital, including photocopying and recording or by any information storage and retrieval system without the prior written permission of both the publisher, Oliver Heber Books and the author, Lexi Post, except in the case of brief quotations embodied in critical articles and reviews.

PUBLISHER'S NOTE: This is a work of fiction. Names, characters, places, and incidents either are the product of the author's imagination or are used fictitiously. Any resemblance to actual persons, living or dead, business establishments, events, or locales is entirely coincidental.

Copyright 2024 © Lexi Post

All rights reserved.

Cover design by Dar Albert

0 9 8 7 6 5 4 3 2 1

ACKNOWLEDGMENTS

For my husband, Bob Fabich, who makes such great meals at home that I have no interest in restaurants, and who fully supports my career and values it as much as I do.

Thank you to my sister, Paige Wood, who is always honest about my stories and happy to help me get them right for my readers.

I had a lot of help from my reader group, *Lexi's Legends*, on this book. Specifically, I'd like to thank Bonnie Davis, RD Pauls, Teresa Fordice, Denise Hasund Sherman, Lenna Hendershott, Lisa Carlton Guertin, Vicki Skinner Fowler, and Bette Read. Also, a special shout out to Patrica Way who took my penchant for ice cream and ran with it for the name of the Dunn's ranch in the most perfect way. As we know, the road to love can be a bit rocky sometimes.

As usual, my sweet and wonderful critique partner, Marie Patrick, was with me every misstep and step of the way, always encouraging and always asking for more.

Lastly, I'd like to thank my agent, Jill Marsal for finding a home for this series. And I want to thank my publisher, Tanya-Ann Crosby, and my editor, Jill Stadler, for making this such a wonderful experience. You ladies rock!

AUTHOR NOTE

This story was inspired by a very old Greek tragedy first performed in 472 BC. Not inspired by the actual story or particular characters, but in the purpose for which it was written. *The Persians* by Aeschylus, is the story of Xerxes, the King of the Persians, who is soundly defeated in the battle of Salamis, where he is the attacker bent on revenge for his country's loss at the battle of Marathon. As this play is a tragedy, that means by definition that the audience is treated to a "hero's" great suffering. What is unique about this is that it was a play preformed for a Greek audience and they were the victors, which causes scholars to hypothesize that the play was meant to generate empathy for the Persians, the Greek's enemy.

In that vein, then what would happen to a woman who enters enemy territory and does indeed empathize with the defeated enemy? Would she then defend her said enemy to her family, attempt a peace, share her knowledge with

AUTHOR NOTE

those willing to further the defeat of their known adversaries or completely switch her loyalty? When love muddies the waters, it is difficult to see what the outcome will be.

CHAPTER 1
FOUR PEAKS, ARIZONA

TANNER DUNN STRODE into the kitchen and headed for the refrigerator. Morning chores were completed and two men were headed for the western border of the ranch. He hated sending two men when they barely had enough as it was, but after his father's stroke out there alone, he wouldn't risk sending only one to ride the fences. Opening the fridge, he grabbed a water bottle.

Brody walked in and sat on a stool at the massive kitchen island. "I'll take one, too."

Tossing his youngest brother the bottle, he closed the fridge. "Is Dad settled in?"

"I guess. It's hard to tell." Brody unscrewed the cap and tossed it into the trash across the kitchen. "That's not Dad in there."

His gut tensed. He'd expected that reaction. "Yes, it is. He just has to get better."

"*If* he can get better."

Tanner swallowed down half the bottle to avoid responding. It was the same thought he'd had when he first saw Dad in the hospital. Seeing his robust, energy-filled father lying in a hospital bed unable to talk or even feed himself had been a shock. At least he was still alive. "He'll get the best care. Dad's a fighter."

"Have you heard from the Town Council? Maybe if Dad knew the dude ranch thing had been approved, it would give him something to fight for."

Personally, he'd been hoping the town *wouldn't* change the zoning that would allow them to become a dude ranch. The last thing he wanted was for Rocky Road Ranch to have a bunch of city people roaming around who didn't know a horse's head from its ass. But he also hadn't figured out what else they could do to save the place. As the oldest, his dad's stroke had added more responsibilities to his shoulders than he'd realized. Unwilling to allow his father to remain in the glorified nursing home called a rehabilitation center, he'd added the care of his dad to the list. He wanted Dad where he could monitor the care he received.

Silently, he swore. If it weren't for Bill Hayden, they wouldn't be close to losing the ranch and his dad probably wouldn't have had a stroke. The Haydens were a greedy bunch, who just couldn't keep their noses out of other people's business.

"Hey, someone just pulled up in a freaking sedan." Brody grinned. "Maybe it's someone from the Town Council. I can't think of anyone else stupid enough to drive out here without a truck. They're going to need a major alignment after this."

His chest tightened, his lungs getting very little air. If it was someone from the town, their whole future was about to change, one way or the other. Leaving the water bottle on the counter, he grabbed his hat off the entry table, strode to the front door of their sprawling single-story adobe home and opened it.

A woman with straight, almost white-blonde hair stepped from the vehicle in a red fitted power suit and black high heels. She bent over, reaching into the car, showing off her very nice ass before she pulled a black leather satchel from the vehicle, threw it over her shoulder, and turned toward him.

It wasn't until he saw her face that his blood boiled. "What the hell are you doing here?" He strode toward her, the large front door slamming behind him.

She narrowed her eyes at him. "I'm your father's physical therapist and speech pathologist."

Over his dead body. He shook his head even as his long stride ate up the distance between them, his boots crunching the desert dirt with each purposeful step. Mandy Hayden didn't look much different than she had in high school. She might have a few more curves and her pert nose had turned sharper, but her blue eyes were still piercing. The only difference was the suit.

Their families had been at odds since he was eight.

The whole town knew it. Even the schools never put a Dunn and a Hayden in the same classroom. He came to a stop three yards from her. "The paperwork they sent home with Dad says he'll have an Amanda Davis treating him, not you. Get off this property. Now."

She gave an exaggerated sigh. "I was married, so Amanda Hayden *Davis*. I haven't changed my name back yet, not that it's your concern."

He snorted. "Guess your husband didn't like having to kowtow to your father. Smart man to get out while he could."

She crossed her arms over her chest. "Must be, since you're such an expert on my father."

He glared at her beneath the shade of his black cowboy hat.

She glared right back. "I'm here to do an assessment of Jeremiah Dunn's physical and speech deficiencies to determine a plan of treatment."

He lifted his arm and pointed beyond her. "Listen, Handy Mandy, I don't give a rat's ass why you say you're here because you're going to hop back in that pretty little sedan of yours and hightail it out of here."

"Handy Mandy? Really? I haven't heard that nickname in over fifteen years. You're still living in the past, Dunn. Guess I'll have to be the mature one here, not that it's that difficult."

He brought his hand down and clenched it. He wasn't going to let her goad him into acting the simpleton. "I said get off my property."

BETWEEN A ROCK AND A COWBOY

"So in other words, you don't care if your father ever walks, or talks, or feeds himself again." She spread one arm out to encompass the property. "I imagine that works well for you, though, since that means this little place is all yours."

Her insinuation that he wanted the place to himself was so far off the mark he would have laughed, but she'd voiced his greatest fear, that Dad would never improve, which felt like being kicked behind the knees. He jerked his chin up. "I'll get someone else."

"There *is* no one else. There's a shortage of therapists in the county, and only three who can do what I do." She cocked her head. "Don't you watch the news?"

"No." He pulled a bandana from his back pocket and lifted his hat to wipe sweat from his brow. It was already over a hundred with no cloud in sight and his anger wasn't helping.

She shuddered as if it were below zero out. "Believe me, I'm no happier about this than you are."

He stuffed the bandana back in his pocket, shaking his head. "We can wait for someone else to be available."

She dropped her arms and put one hand on her hip. "Three months?"

"What?"

"I said three months. That's how long you'd have to wait before your father could get a therapist." She threw her free hand up. "Of course, by then his muscles would have settled into comfortable disfunction. He'd probably need therapy for the rest of his life at that point."

Once again, his stomach tensed as his fear intensified. "You don't know that."

She raised her brows. "Actually, I do. I read his file. Jeremiah Dunn suffered a massive stroke, and to make matters worse, he was out on his horse when it happened. Not only did he fall, but he wasn't found for three hours. That made it impossible to give him TPA. You may not like it. I may not like it. But I'm your father's best chance at being able to function again."

Function? The word sounded ominous. What about getting his father back to the way he was, riding the property, instructing the ranch hands, yelling at him to stop leaving water bottles all over the house?

At that moment, the front door opened behind him and the crunch of his brother's boots followed.

Brody reached him, a stupid smile on his face. "Appears we have company."

Mandy Hayden returned the smile. "I'm Amanda Davis, your father's physical therapist and speech pathologist."

Brody stepped forward. "I'm Brody. It's nice to—"

"She's a Hayden." Tanner spat on the ground. Just saying her name put a bad taste in his mouth.

Brody halted and looked back at him. "What?"

"This is Handy Mandy."

Brody looked at him then back at her. "Oh. Last time I saw you was in high school. You were in a wheelchair. You've changed."

She rolled her eyes. "Well, it has been over ten years since I was in high school."

"Yeah, she got married to a Mr. Davis." He didn't keep the sneer out of his voice. How anyone would want to marry into the Hayden family was beyond him. Then again, her dad was a state rep, so maybe her ex married her for politics, one of those assholes who only wanted money and power. It took one to know one. Probably never worked an honest day in his life.

"Davis, Davis." Brody's brow furrowed. "Do you mean that lawyer who represented the developer who wanted to turn half the New River conservation land into vacation rentals?"

A red blush to match her suit crept from the v of her blouse, up her neck, to infuse her entire face. "Yes, he's the one."

Now that was interesting. Was she embarrassed because she'd married Davis or because he lost the case?

"What an asshole."

At Brody's exclamation, she nodded. "Just one of the many reasons why I divorced him."

Enough of the chitchat. "Ms. Davis was just leaving."

"No, Ms. Davis was just coming." She held her hands up as if he held her at gunpoint. "Unless of course you don't want your father to improve."

She needed to stop saying that. "If there's no one else, we can always bring him for his therapy." He clapped a hand on brother's shoulder. "Brody's always in a hurry to get off the ranch."

His brother pulled away.

"Every day?" She was back to crossing her arms. "He'll have to be taken into Scottsdale or Phoenix, your choice, at least six times a week."

There was no way they could spare someone that many days, but he had her now. "I thought you said you were here to make an assessment and develop a plan. If you haven't done either, you don't know what he needs. He may only need therapy a few times a week."

She gave him a smug smile. "You forget, I'm a specialist, and one of the few who can provide two therapies for a patient. I read Jeremiah's file. He's going to need daily therapy and a lot of it. I need to assess him to determine what we need to work on first and what needs the most attention, as well as how long he'll need before there is nothing more to do. So are you going to let me do my job or keep your father incapacitated?"

"Tanner." Brody's whispered word held a wealth of meaning.

He hated what he had to do with his entire being, but his father *had* to get better. "Fine."

She grinned and started forward.

He held up his hand. "But under two conditions."

She stopped, her eyes narrowing again. "What conditions?"

"First, if my father recognizes you, you leave. I don't want him having another stroke because a Hayden is in *his* house."

She looked away, obviously pondering his words.

Finally, she nodded. "I agree. I'm here to help my patient. If my presence causes harm, then it defeats the purpose. What's your other condition?"

"I approve all therapy."

She laughed. "You're joking, right?"

"Do I look like I'm joking?" He would not be gainsaid on this. He wanted to know everything she did and everywhere she went while on their property. For all he knew, she'd volunteered for this job to feed information to her father so he could put the final nail in the coffin of what was once a thriving cattle operation.

"Not to be insulting, though that is a perk, but you don't have a clue what therapy is right for your father. So what good would that do?"

He stared straight into her eyes. "I know my father better than anyone."

Her eyes rounded at that and she opened her mouth to argue.

"He's right." Brody nodded. "And I can tell you, he's not going to budge on that."

She took a deep breath as if she were counting to ten and slowly let it out. Then she deliberately walked toward him, her hips swaying in her ridiculous high heels until she stood two feet from him. "Fine."

With that, she stepped around him and headed toward the house. He and Brody turned to watch.

"Well, are you going to watch her, or just let her spy on everything in the house?" Brody raised his brow in question.

Tanner slapped him on the back. "Glad to see you understand the problem. Now go show her where Dad is. If there is any sign of recognition, you haul her out of there faster than her tiny high heels can carry her."

"No kidding. She's a rancher's daughter. She should know better than to show up here in those."

They walked toward the house where Amanda Hayden stood waiting. Tanner lowered his voice. "She's also a lawyer's wife. Or ex-wife. I'm sure old habits die hard."

His brother opened the door and Handy Mandy stepped inside, Brody following.

He raised his voice to a more normal volume. "I want a full report when she leaves."

"You got it." His brother doffed his hat and strode forward quickly.

Tanner stepped into the cool entry and dropped his hat on the side table as well.

As his brother entered the kitchen, he could hear her voice. Just what he needed, something else to add to his list of responsibilities. Maybe a call into the agency could get him someone else. No reason to take her word for it.

Turning on his heel, he strode down the hall to his father's office to find the hospital paperwork. If he was lucky, today would be the first and last day Amanda Hayden was ever on Rocky Road Ranch.

Amanda stepped into the Dunn's kitchen from seeing her patient, her heels clicking on the travertine floor. Moving a half-empty water bottle aside on the kitchen island, she dropped her satchel on the butcherblock surface. There were four stools at the counter. She angled her butt onto one and pulled her form-fitted skirt down as far as it would go, which was not far in her position.

At least she was alone with no one watching her every move. Brody Dunn must feel comfortable letting her in the kitchen alone. Guess he didn't worry about her stealing the silver. She smirked, scanning the large predominantly stone and wood kitchen. That was if they even *had* silver. Everything about the house made it clear only men lived in it. No doubt, silver would bend too easily in their bulky hands.

Pulling her ultra-thin laptop from her bag, she added a few more notes to her therapy planner. Jeremiah Dunn was not in good shape, but she'd seen worse, and if he was as stubborn as his oldest son, he'd be improving daily. She'd only had to walk into the converted den to see that Tanner wanted his father to get better.

Actually, a better description for what the room used to be would be *man cave*. The extra-large TV mounted on the wall and the small bar in the corner, now devoid of any alcohol, bottles, or glasses, attested to what it used to be. Now, the entire room was outfitted with therapy equipment. It was a home therapist's dream, even if some of it would be of no help to her patient. Someone had done some research. It also confirmed her father's observation that the Dunns were all about themselves. That may well be, but in this case, it made her job easier.

She was satisfied with the space, which in itself was a rarity. She could be very picky when it came to helping her patients. With Jeremiah, there had been no recognition in his eyes when he'd finally looked at her. That could be because of the stroke or it could simply be because he hadn't seen her since she was little.

She grew up knowing who all the Dunns were. Her dad had made sure of that, but she was probably of no consequence to the patriarch of the Dunn family. While that rubbed her the wrong way, it was very helpful in her new role as his therapist. He did seem to recognize Brody and even Isaac, the certified nurse's aide, which was a plus in his favor. She typed in that note.

Brody was still in with his father, and she had no idea where the third brother was. She was just happy that Tanner wasn't about so she could do her job. She didn't know much about his younger brothers, since they had been behind her in school, but Tanner had been in her grade. Her brothers could probably shed some light on the younger Dunns since they had been closer to their age, not that it really mattered. As long as they stayed out of her way, she could care less where they were or what they did.

"Fuck!"

The exclamation startled her, and she pivoted around toward the large archway at the end of the open concept kitchen-family room. Footsteps sounded from the opposite side of the house. Soon they reached the end of the hall that led to the communal space and Tanner halted. "Looks like I'm stuck with you."

By the sight of his lowered brows and tense jaw, she could see he was pissed to discover that what she'd told him was true. She was his father's only hope. That had to rankle. She shook her head. "Didn't believe me, did you?"

He continued into the room, walked behind the island, and grabbed up the water bottle. "Why should I? Your family isn't exactly known for telling the truth. Haven't met a single politician...or lawyer who did." He unscrewed the cap and took a swallow, a challenge clear in his green eyes.

Irritation burned through her, but she refused to stoop to his level. She was the professional here. He was a cowboy, like her brothers and half the town. "Well, from what I was told, you asked for the best, so now you're stuck with me."

He choked on the water and started coughing.

Medical alarms went off in her head, but if he was coughing, he was breathing. She forced herself to stay still.

Eventually, he finished his coughing fit and took another sip of water before wiping his eyes on the sleeve of his light-blue and white checkered shirt. "Believe me, I never would have expected a Hayden to be the best at anything."

They could throw barbs at each other all day. It wouldn't change a thing. "That's your shortsightedness. But look at the bright side."

He raised one eyebrow. "There's a bright side to my

father having a massive stroke, falling off his horse, lying there for hours, and then getting you for a therapist?"

"Yes, there is. The bright side is I'm the best, and I will get your father as close to normal as his body will allow him to be. So you can first, realize how important he is to you, and second, be grateful you have him back at all."

A pained look crossed his face before he turned his gaze to replacing the cap on the water bottle. "Yeah."

Confused, and not a little curious, she forced herself to ignore him. Saving her final notes, she closed her laptop and stuffed it in her satchel. "I'll be back tomorrow morning. Isaac said he'll be getting your father up at seven, so I'll arrive around nine to give them time for washing, dressing, and feeding."

"You make him sound like he's a chore."

She stilled at the growled words. Digging deep down, she tried to sympathize, and with anyone else she would have, but she was only human. "Until I can find out how far your father can come, he is a chore." She slipped off the stool and pulled her bag off the counter before looking him in the eye. "And you'd best remember that. He can do nothing for himself right now. He's completely dependent on you and the experts you hire. So if you want to see him improve, you help us, or we'll just be wasting our time and your money."

Not waiting to see what he thought about that, she turned on her heel and strode for the door. Just as she opened it, she heard him mumble in the kitchen.

"You're the chore."

Grinning, she closed the door behind her and continued to her car. "Well, that went better than expected." Getting in her now boiling hot vehicle, she tossed her satchel on the passenger seat, turned the ignition, and blasted the air conditioner. Hot air hit her face and she turned her head. Opening the glove box, she pulled out a dish towel and laid it over the steering wheel before putting the vehicle into drive.

Drive, though, was rather optimistic for what she did as the car crawled along the ridiculously rocky road that was the ranch's driveway. There were machines that could fix it, but she could imagine Jeremiah Dunn refusing to spend money on the mile-long drive just so it could live up to its name. Men could be such stubborn, mule-headed, stupid creatures sometimes that she wondered how civilization had evolved as far as it had.

It didn't take much observation to see that Tanner Dunn had not fallen far from his father's family tree branch. If Tanner was that bad, how bad would Jeremiah be? Her one hope was that the stroke had changed Jeremiah's personality enough to make it possible for her to get through to him.

As far as the tall, dark-haired, and much broader Tanner than the boy she remembered from school was concerned, he was on his own. She had no intention of dealing with him any more than she had to. His welcome was exactly what she'd expected. He'd always held a confidence and physicality that the girls in high school swooned over. Arrogant was the label she'd given him, but she'd forgotten his penetrating green gaze, having only looked him in the eyes a couple times way back when. But he'd been a mere teenager then.

Now he was a grown man and an impressive one at that. Not only had he filled out, but his jaw had become more defined, and she'd bet a month's salary he sported six-pack abs. His personality, despite her jabs, had matured as well. He had a dynamic and forcefulness about him as if what he said was law. She'd bet none of his men ever attempted lying to him about why they got to work late, if they dared to come in late at all.

She couldn't let her guard down. Going soft on him, like she usually did with the family members of her clients, could be dangerous. Keeping him off balance was the only way she could get her work done. He probably still thought he was above her simply because he was a man. She grinned. She'd have to substitute some of the layman's terms for the medical ones in the rehabilitation plan before giving him a copy. Let him know he was out of his depth when it came to—

Her phone rang, and she pressed the car Bluetooth speaker. "Hello."

"Hey, Amanda, how'd it go? Did he have you arrested? Escorted off the property? Keep you away at gun point?"

Only LaReina, her supervisor and mentor, would joke about her visit. Since the woman was from Phoenix, she was clueless about small-town living. "No, but he did tell me to get the hell off his property."

"Really?" The pause only lasted seconds. "But you got him to accept you, right? Did you use your usual charm?"

She laughed. "Hardly. I told you. This feud goes way back. I stood my ground and told him what his options were. He didn't like any of them. I was his last choice because I was his only choice."

"I knew you could do it. Though, I admit I was worried when I heard he'd called the office."

Good, she was glad LaReina had some doubts. She certainly hadn't been confident arriving at Rocky Road. "Did you sign the paperwork for my sabbatical?" That had been their deal. She'd thought being both a physical therapist and a speech pathologist would give her flexibility with her schedule. It had done the opposite, making her in demand more than almost anyone else, which meant very little time off, what she valued more than gold. Something else LaReina didn't truly understand.

"Not yet. I had to be sure you were actually going to be able to get onto that ranch and do the job."

"I can do the job. Sign the paperwork and send me an electronic copy."

"You do realize I'm your supervisor, right?"

"I do." She stuck her tongue out at her dashboard where LaReina's voice came through. "And you understand that I'm just as happy to walk to get that time off."

A heavy sigh came through the speaker. "Yeah, I know. Don't worry. I'll sign it."

"Good." Suddenly the whole car tilted and shook. "Crap."

"What is it? Everything okay? Where are you, anyway?"

She stopped the car. Driving and talking on such a treacherous drive just didn't work. "I'm leaving Rocky Road Ranch and I just bottomed out. I have to go. I'll talk to you tomorrow and give you a full report after you get the assessment and plan."

"Sounds good. Talk to you *mañana*." With that, LaReina ended the call.

Focusing on the road, she eased the car up out of the rut she'd driven into. She would need an alignment after this. Dressing to impress hadn't even worked. She should have brought one of her father's trucks and come in a comfortable pair of jeans and boots. As it was, she'd have to go through a car wash on the way back to her dad's place. She wasn't taking any chances her father would figure out who her client was. If he discovered it was Jermiah who needed physical and speech therapy from her, it could violate HIPAA regulations and get her fired, never mind piss her father off royally.

She really needed to find a place of her own. She'd only meant to move back to the family homestead for a few weeks after the divorce, but then there was the sale of the house she'd owned with Claude, and the final settlement details, and now she'd been at home two months. She toyed with renting a place, but she'd rather spend the money on experiences. The bigger problem was, she didn't want to waste her limited free time looking for somewhere to live.

Finally, she passed under the sign designating the

ranch as Rocky Road, though it also served as a warning to unsuspecting visitors. Pulling onto a dirt road that would lead to a real road and Main Street, she relaxed. The graded road required far less attention.

This weekend was out for house hunting since she was flying to Vegas with friends. Next weekend was barrel race exhibition practice for Pioneer Days on the one day she'd have off.

She simply didn't have time. *Delegate. Delegate. Delegate.* Her ex-husband's voice echoed in her head like a grackle excited over a potato chip. He'd never understood why she couldn't hand off her work to someone else. That was because she actually did her own work. But in this case, he might just have a point. She'd check into real-estate agents in town. There was bound to be someone from high school who had gone into that field. Happy with her plan, she pulled onto the paved Black Spur Road and was soon headed for town.

Four Peaks used to be small, but it had grown along with every other space in Arizona. It now had a few chain stores and even three grocers, but compared to living in Phoenix, it still felt small to her. After a quick car wash and a stop in the local coffee shop for a skinny mocha latte, she headed to Cholla Valley. She should have the whole ranch house to herself. Her father was in Phoenix and her brothers should be out with the cattle.

In no time, she was parking her sedan next to the two pickup trucks parked out front. She unfolded herself from the car and grabbed her satchel. She should probably think about buying a truck, but that depended on where she decided to live. Now that she was free of Claude Davis, she had so many more options, none of which needed to impress clients. Slamming the driver's side door unintentionally, she walked down the path of pavers set among the green grass that made a front yard. It was a bit out of place in the desert landscape, but it had been a requirement of her mother's, who now lived in Washington, DC with her third husband.

Stepping onto the covered porch of the four-thousand-foot hacienda, she reached for the door, but it opened before she could touch it.

"Oh, I didn't know you were there." The pale, petite, black-haired woman appeared confused.

Great, just what she needed, another girlfriend of one of her brothers. "Who are you?"

"I'm Twilight." The woman scowled. "Who are you? Are you here for Luke?"

Amanda barely kept from rolling her eyes. "No, he's my brother."

Twilight scrunched up her face as she tried to figure out what that meant. Suddenly, her brown eyes widened. "Oh, you're his sister. He didn't tell me he had a sister."

That was surprising since her brothers liked to complain about her quite a lot, especially since she'd moved back home. "How long have you known my brother?"

"We met last night." Twilight wiggled her dark eyebrows. "He's quite a dancer."

Lovely, a one-night stand...hopefully. "Were you leaving?"

Twilight's eyes widened again. "Oh yes. I have to get home and showered. My boyfriend is taking me to a concert tonight. It's my birthday."

She certainly hoped Luke knew what he was doing with Miss Twilight, but she doubted it. He seemed to go out of his way to get into tough situations. "Well, I'll let you go. Happy birthday."

As the woman stood in the doorway smiling, it appeared she hadn't figured out that she needed to exit.

Done with the conversation, Amanda stepped forward and opened the door wider. "Bye."

Twilight finally moved. "Bye. Have a nice day."

Closing the door behind her, she dropped her satchel on the side table next to it and kicked off her heels, the cool air reviving her. "Now that's better."

The door opened behind her and hit her on the butt, causing her to stumble.

Twilight walked in. "Forgot my keys." She shrugged before walking through the entry and back into the house.

Part of her wanted to introduce Twilight to Claude. She was exactly what the man had always wanted. Someone cute and brainless. In a way, he was much like her mother. He married to help his career, and when he got everything he could from their marriage, he moved on. He hadn't counted on her having the best divorce lawyer in Maricopa County. It was one time when she'd been happy for her father's connections.

She grabbed up her shoes and bag then walked in the opposite direction of Miss Twilight. Having set up her home office in the old guest room next to her room, she dropped her satchel on the couch then stepped into her room and started to strip. Thankful to get out of the form-fitted clothes, she pulled on a pair of jeans and a sleeveless button-down shirt and moved back into her office.

Now to fill out her plan for Jeremiah. As she pulled her laptop out and set it on the desk, she mentally went through names of good occupational therapists that might like some extra cash. Sitting down, she set about rereading the original plan from the hospital and adding her own pieces to the puzzle. She stilled at the sound of the front door closing before she remembered it must be Twilight leaving. Even so, she closed her laptop and listened.

The familiar sound of cowboy boots on the tiled floors made it clear it wasn't Twilight. She must not have heard the woman leave. Quickly, she left the room and closed the door. Walking into the living room, she found her father reading a message on his phone in front of the wall-to-wall river-rock fireplace. He was dressed in his usual khakis and sport shirt. He always said it made him appear more approachable to his constituents. Despite having a good cook, he was still lean around the middle, but more white was sprinkling his light-brown hair in addition to the distinguished patches at his temples. "You're home?"

He turned at her voice. "Yes. I only had one meeting today. I was surprised to see your car parked out front. Your patient must live close."

She flopped onto the Italian leather loveseat. "Dad, no fishing."

He held his hands out. "What? Can't a father be concerned about his daughter's commute?"

She would have taken him seriously, but his gray eyes were definitely smiling. "You know I can't tell you who my *client* is. That's against regulations." And all hell would break lose if he found out.

He snapped his phone back into the holder at his waist. "You have to admit, you weren't gone half a day."

She folded her legs under her. Could he really be interested in what she did? "That's because today was just introductions and a quick assessment. I'll spend the rest of the afternoon putting together two plans, one for physical therapy and one for speech. Then I'm sure there will be calls with the doctor to get everything approved. I'll start..." She didn't bother to continue. She could see her father had already lost interest, his gaze having wandered toward the full wall of folding glass doors that looked out onto their pool. "Later, I'll probably look into places to live."

That caught his interest. He snapped his attention back to her. "Why do you have to do that when you have a perfectly good place right here?"

She rolled her eyes. "Because I'm twenty-nine and need my own space."

"I can have your brother move to the west wing and then you'd have almost half the house to yourself." He walked over to the side of the loveseat where she sat. "You know I like having my girl home."

She swallowed hard at his phrasing. That's what he'd said to her when she'd come home from the hospital and couldn't do a damn thing for herself. She reached up and took his hand. "I know, Dad. I promise not to look too hard." She squeezed and winked.

He squeezed her hand back before letting go. "You always were my favorite child."

She was quite sure he said that to all his kids when he was alone with them, but even so, it did make her feel good. "And you're my favorite parent."

He puffed with pride at that. "Of course." He chuckled. "I need to get in a swim before my next meeting. It's online, so I'll be in my office and out of your hair."

She uncrossed her legs and stood. "No problem. I'll be in my office, too."

He started walking toward his room in the east wing then stopped. "By the way, there's that odd-flavored ice cream you like in the freezer. I got it just for you."

She was quite sure their cook picked it up, but the fact he'd thought of her warmed her heart. "Thanks. I'll have some after dinner for sure."

He smiled then continued toward his room.

She strolled back to her office. In some ways, it was good to be home again. Sitting at her desk, she opened her computer. As the warm fuzzies she'd gotten from talking with her dad wore off, reality set in.

Just to be safe, she'd change her password. The last thing she wanted was for any of her family to know she was working in enemy territory because that's exactly how they would look at it. It was how *she* looked at it. But unlike her three younger brothers, she was a professional.

So why did she have a sinking feeling in her stomach that this wasn't going to end well? She shook herself. That was silly. She'd do her job and leave. No one would be the wiser.

CHAPTER 2

"I BABYSAT HER LAST TIME." Brody shook his head as he walked from the stable to the house. "It's your turn."

Tanner stood at the front door and watched the dust cloud in the distance, a sure sign that Amanda Hayden was about to descend upon the ranch again. Every ounce of his being rebelled. "I don't have that kind of time."

"Well, I don't either. And I doubt even if Jackson were home that he'd have time either. We're shorthanded as it is."

He wiped the sweat from his brow, desperately trying to think of a solution. He refused to let the woman have the run of the house while they were out working. Unfortunately, Isaac had time off until dinner on Tuesdays, so it would be just her and Dad, not an acceptable option.

Brody turned away from the driveway and faced him. "Why don't we set up some cameras?"

"Cameras?" He frowned. "You mean like spy on Dad? No. I'm not stooping that low."

His brother threw his hands up in exasperation. "You can't have everything. Either we set up cameras or you stay here twiddling your thumbs while you stare at her." Brody stilled. "Or is that what you want to do? She's certainly a better sight than your bovine sweetheart, Lulubell."

"Fuck you." He turned back to the house, Brody's steps following.

"It was a legit question. When I first saw Amanda, I thought she was attractive, until I learned who she was."

He opened the door, ignoring his brother. He'd noticed too, which just pissed him off more. People as greedy as the Haydens should look hungry or cruel or something to forewarn others. Not her. In her tailored suit with the short skirt, she looked like a damn model. He'd never seen a woman in Four Peaks with legs that long.

"Her looks could be helpful."

He walked into the kitchen and pulled open the dishwasher to throw the dirty coffee mugs inside. He scowled at his brother, who remained in the opening that separated the entry from the main room. "I see them only as a detriment."

"Sure, *you* do. But Dad will have a pretty face to look at during his therapy. Maybe it'll help."

Sometimes Brody's attempts at humor really pissed him off. He pointed toward the hallway and scowled. "Just go order those cameras. We'll put them in all the rooms but Dad's. Have them here by tomorrow. I can't afford to lose another day of work."

Brody's smile faltered. "You do know that even overnight shipping is never overnight out here, right?"

He closed the dishwasher and dried his hands on a towel before hanging it back on its hook. "Just get them here ASAP because after today, you're babysitting."

"I'm on it." Brody disappeared down the hall to the office.

At least his brother was a whiz at ordering supplies. It was one less thing for him to do. Now what he had to do was let his father know his therapy would start today. Walking through the stone arch between the kitchen and the old den, he found Isaac buttoning the final button on Dad's collared shirt. "Leave the top two open."

"What?" Isaac looked up. He was a tall man, which was probably to his advantage when moving clients. He had a shaved head and a tattoo just barely visible under his sleeve. He'd come highly recommended.

Unfortunately, so had Amanda. "Leave the top two buttons undone. Dad wears his buttoned shirts like that."

"Oh, good to know. Thanks."

Tanner walked to the small table that seated four, pulled a straight back chair away from it and straddled it to face his dad. His gut tensed as he noted his dad's white shirt with the embroidered horses was loose on him, and it didn't go with his sweatpants. His large, square head looked too big for his body. It was a weird sight, especially for a man who had always been muscular and in the last few years had grown a bit around his middle. There was no middle anymore. Even Dad's nose seemed smaller and his expressive green eyes, so much like his own, lacked their usual liveliness.

Issac patted Dad's bony shoulder. "Okay, we are almost ready for our company. Would you like me to comb your hair?" Not waiting for an answer, the nursing assistant walked into the bedroom.

So Isaac had already told Dad about Amanda. "Is that why you're all gussied up? For your therapist?"

His dad shrugged, but only one side lifted.

He resented the fancy shirt preparation. He couldn't very well tell Dad that Amanda was a Hayden, and therefore, not worthy of dressing up for, no matter how pretty she was. "Mrs. Davis is going to be helping you with your physical abilities and your speech."

His father grunted, staring at him with no expression.

"I think Mr. Dunn is going to do very well." Isaac walked back in and started combing the too long strands of hair. "I read the report from the hospital. He's very good at working hard to get better."

An odd look crossed Dad's face.

Tanner only noticed because he hadn't seen many expressions at all. Something about it had him tensing. "Dad has always worked hard, but he can be stubborn."

His father's gaze drifted away. Was that on purpose or couldn't he help it? Damn, he wished he knew more about strokes and even more, wished his father could talk to him.

"So Tanner, what do you think. Is he presentable?"

At Isaac's question, he pretended to consider, not wanting his dad to know that he looked like a shadow of his old self. "Definitely a handsome dude. Must be where I got my looks from."

That elicited another grunt, but his dad's thin shoulders did seem to straighten a bit.

The chimes from the doorbell rang, and he quickly rose, spinning the chair around and setting it back under the table. "That must be Mrs. Davis." He strode from the room, an unexpected feeling of hope rising in his chest, which he tamped down quickly. He'd barely made it halfway across the kitchen before she stepped into it.

"Good morning. How's your father this morning?"

Taken aback not only by her entrance into the house but also by her scrubs, sneakers, and ponytail, he frowned. "You couldn't wait until I let you in?"

She smiled as she walked around him and set her black bag on the kitchen island. "No. I'm going to be here every day, six days a week, starting next week. There's no need for you or anyone else to let me in. You can go about your daily activities as usual unless I need you, in which case, I'll call." She pulled paperwork from her bag.

She was shorter in her sneakers and much more approachable, though the scrubs put him off. Ever since talking to the doctor at the hospital where the ambulance had taken his father, people in scrubs made him feel powerless, and he despised that feeling. But he wasn't powerless because she was on *his* ranch and she was a Hayden.

"I found your number in the hospital files and added it to my phone." She raised her hand as if he was about to argue. "Don't worry. As soon as I fulfill my contract, I'll erase it."

He hadn't thought that far ahead. He'd barely thought beyond her arriving today. He needed to get his head in the game. "For today, I'll be hanging around."

Her brows lowered, but she didn't say anything, just went back to shuffling her papers. Pulling a packet from the pile, she held it out. "Here you go."

"What's that?"

"This is your father's therapy plan. You said you wanted to approve everything. The first part is for his physical therapy. The second half is for his speech therapy. I also took the liberty of contacting an excellent occupational therapist. She comes with the package you bought from my employer, so no need to worry about an added expense."

"I don't put money before my father." The words came out in almost a growl, and he swallowed hard. If anyone else had made that comment, he could have answered civilly, but coming from a Hayden, it crossed a line.

Her eyes widened. "I meant no disrespect. I inform all my clients of services that are included and make requests for additional ones only if they are absolutely needed. You did want the plan, correct?"

Since she still held the papers out, he took them from her.

"To put it briefly, I'm going to start at the level he was before he left the hospital. I'm expecting good strides of improvement in the beginning and then it will become slower as time progresses."

As she laid out her plans for his father's rehabilitation, he lost track. It sounded like another language to him, the kind the doctor had spoken when he'd told him what had happened to his father. Something about blood clots and brain cells dying. He felt completely stupid and out of his element. The feeling was too reminiscent of when he lost his brother. He didn't have time for feelings. He had a ranch to run.

"Does that make sense?"

He nodded, lifting the sheet of papers. "It will probably make more sense after I read these." He set the papers down on the island and lowered his voice. "I told my father that Mrs. Davis was his therapist. I want to stay away from your first name to avoid recognition."

Her brow furrowed and she pulled her lips in. "Hmmm. I'm afraid I already told him I was Amanda yesterday." She kept her voice low as well. "I think if we stay away from my childhood name of Mandy, we should be okay."

He didn't like it, but what choice did he have? It felt more and more like his father's health was in the hands of others, and he didn't like that either. "If at any time he figures out who you are, you are to leave immediately. Do you understand?" Though his voice was barely above a whisper, he gave it the force he needed.

She took a step back and straightened her shoulders. "I assure you, I put my patients' needs first. Always."

He'd pissed her off, but he didn't care. As long as his message was heard. "Good. Since we are agreed, you may proceed." He held his arm out toward the den.

Her lips thinned and she gave him a scowl, but she refrained from speaking. Instead, she left her bag on the island and walked into the den.

He moved around the counter to sit on a stool, pulled the paperwork toward him, and started reading, his ears trained on the conversation going on between Isaac and Amanda. His father's every move was discussed in what to him was an invasion of privacy. It wasn't as if his dad's hearing had been affected.

Finally, the conversation stopped and Isaac came out. "I'm heading out. I'll be back by four to get his dinner ready."

"Let me walk you out."

Isaac raised his eyebrows, but nodded, and they strode out together.

Once outside, he stopped. "I know that communicating my father's activities and progress is important between all of you. But I'd prefer that you don't do it in front of him. His hearing is fine and talking about him in front of him is demeaning."

Isaac put his hand on his shoulder. "You do know that your father will never be the same person he was, right?"

He stepped away, dislodging the man's hand. "I know he may not return to his same physical capabilities, yes."

Isaac shook his head. "I'm talking about his personality.

Many times, a stroke victim's personality changes dependent on what parts of the brain were affected."

He swallowed hard. He hadn't been told that. "That may be true, but he can still hear and no matter what type of person he is now, I don't want him talked about as if he isn't there."

"Sometimes patients prefer us to not hide things from them, but you're the boss. I'll be sure to keep further communications with the other medical staff out of range of his hearing."

Relieved that his father would continue to be treated like a person, even if he was a stroke *victim*, he gave Isaac a nod. "Thank you."

As Isaac walked off, Tanner remained. What did his father's personality have to do with anything? He watched the man's small pickup truck head down the drive before returning to the house. When he entered the kitchen, he ignored the paperwork and continued into the den to find his father squeezing a ball, or trying to.

"Excellent. Now I want you to do the same with your other hand." Amanda took the palm-sized ball and placed it in his father's other hand.

His father started to squeeze it. This time his fingers buried deep into the ball's surface.

"That hand is even better." Amanda smiled.

His father squeezed then suddenly looked directly at him and stopped.

"That was only five. Come on. Give me five more."

His dad's hand didn't move, but he returned his gaze to Amanda.

"Now Jeremiah, we talked about this. You can't favor one side over the other. I need five more squeezes."

His father let go of the ball altogether and it rolled across the table. Amanda caught it just as it went off the side. That's when she noticed him. "Can we help you, Tanner?"

"No, I'm fine."

She turned back to his father. "I know, he's such a distraction. Just ignore the dragon in the archway." She placed the ball next to his father's right hand.

His dad looked back at him. There was a slight lift to his chin.

It was the tiniest of movement, but it struck a chord in him. *That* was his dad. He always did that just as he dug in his heels about something. A slice of joy shot through him. His dad was still there!

Amanda rose. "Tanner, I need a word with you."

Since his father still stared at him, he gave an exaggerated sigh. "Very well." He turned back into the kitchen, but walked past the island and farther into the family room so they couldn't be overheard.

Amanda's sneakers made little sound on the tiled floor as she followed, but he was very aware she was there. "You can't watch."

He spun at her softly spoken words. "Excuse me?"

She crossed her arms over her chest. "I said you can't watch his therapy."

Affronted, he took a step toward her and pointed toward the old den. "That's my father in there, and this is *my* house. I can do whatever the blazes I feel like doing."

"No, you can't. Not if you want your father to make progress."

He dropped his arm, laying his hand on the back of the large armchair his dad used to sit in after dinner. Though he knew she was right, it rankled too much. He wanted to cheer his father on, not ignore him.

"He doesn't want you watching him."

His heart seemed to stop at that. Having his instincts confirmed hit a nerve. Did Dad blame him as much as he blamed himself?

She unfolded her arms and put her hand on his. "This is not about you. He has his pride. He doesn't like you seeing him like this. You need to let him make some progress first."

Her touch, so foreign, yet so comforting, had him pulling away. He didn't want to feel anything from a Hayden. "And you know all this when you don't even know him?" He lifted an eyebrow, not willing to let her know how uncomfortable she made him.

She gave him a sympathetic smile. "But I do. I know what this is like for my patients because I went through something similar."

At her reference to knowing what it was like, a flashback from high school swept through his mind of her in a wheelchair rolling down the hallway. He'd forgotten. All kinds of rumors flew around school from a drunk driver to falling off a horse.

"Patients like your father are embarrassed because they know what they were like before and how weak and pathetic they are now, and it hurts. Not in a pain way but psychologically. For the head of a household to be laid so low is beyond what his psyche can cope with. So you need to give him some time."

He just wanted his dad back, but that was obviously never going to happen. Even as the thought filled his head, he rejected it. "Fine. I have stuff I need to do in the barn." Not caring what she thought of his sudden capitulation, he turned on his heel and strode out the front door even as his chest tightened and his eyes grew moist.

Kicking up dust as he headed for the large stables, he gritted his teeth. His dad *would* get better, and if Handy Mandy couldn't make that happen then he'd just find someone who could. He stopped in the shade of the open doors, the scent of hay, horse, and leather calming his emotions.

Since his mom died, it had been him, Jackson, Brody, and his dad. He wasn't ready for that to change. He'd been trained to take over Rocky Road, he just hadn't expected to do so twenty years early, and certainly not when the fate of the ranch was up in the air.

There was far too much work to be done to be overseeing his dad's care when there were trained professionals on the job. If anyone else had been assigned as his dad's physical therapist, he would be out on the range right now, not cooling his heels in the barn.

Yesterday, when Mandy Hayden showed up on his doorstep, it had been easy to tell her to leave. Today in her damn scrubs, sneakers, ponytail, sympathetic looks, and kind touch, she seemed almost human. He didn't want her to be human. He just needed her to do her job.

His job was to keep the ranch viable until Dad could take the reins again. *If* he could take the reins. His father was only fifty-two. He was still young. His body could still recover.

Nodding to himself, he strode into the barn. He hadn't planned on mucking out stalls all morning, but if it kept him from being around his dad's physical therapist, then he was happy to do it. He grabbed the shavings fork and the wheelbarrow then yanked open a stall. But as he attacked it with fury, he kept feeling her hand on his and he rubbed the back of his glove as if he could erase the memory.

It had to be because she was a woman, and he hadn't been with a woman or on a date in far too long. He had too many responsibilities to add a relationship to his list. That was probably why he kept thinking about Amanda's round blue eyes, bright smile, and seductive curves. She'd changed so much from the thin waif she'd been in high school that he was surprised he'd recognized her yesterday. Then again, her heart-shaped face really hadn't changed even if her body had. What he hadn't expected was her kindness. As far as he was concerned, that trait could be deadly.

Nope, he wasn't going back inside until it was time to give Dad his lunch. Nope, he wasn't going no matter what.

Amanda shook her head. "Are you flirting with me?"

Another smile formed on Jeremiah's face.

"Yes, I know you can do the smiles and the puckers. But you need to practice touching your nose and chin with your tongue tonight."

The man puckered.

Despite her best efforts, Jeremiah was picking and choosing what he wanted to do. It had been like this for over a week now. It was as if he didn't take his recovery seriously and just liked having her around for company.

Her mind halted. Was that it? He didn't take his recovery seriously? Her heart squeezed. She'd always been able to read her patients, knowing what it was like to be unable to make their minds and bodies work like they wanted them to. Depression was common, but she hadn't seen that in Jeremiah at all.

He stopped puckering his lips and stared at her. There was no sparkle in his eye like when he was teasing her. It was his dead-man's gaze where he looked as if he could see the beyond and wanted to go there.

"Fine, no more tongue exercises for now."

His green gaze returned to her and focused once again. Then he stuck his tongue out at her.

She widened her eyes in shock before laughing, ignoring the sound of the front door opening. "That's about as mature as the teenager who was on my sunrise hot-air-balloon ride this morning. He thought doing spitballs over the basket was fun." She rolled her eyes at what an ass the kid had been, but his mother had been too busy flirting with the balloon operator to notice.

Jeremiah shrugged, his shoulders a little closer to lifting evenly than they had been last week...a little.

She had to figure out how to get him to do *all* his therapy sooner rather than later. "It was an amazing view. Arizona sunrises are almost as beautiful as its sunsets. My next balloon ride is a sunset. Do you ever watch the sunrise?"

He grunted.

She'd learned that meant he had more to say but wasn't about to try. Actually, he had three grunts. There was that one. One was a reply like "wiseass." The other she was still deciding on.

Footsteps sounded across the kitchen and from the cadence she knew them to be Tanner's. He had a purposeful stride while Brody's steps sounded more like he was moving only because he had to, probably because he was far less comfortable around his father and didn't look forward to their lunches together.

Ignoring the man in the other room, who most likely had come in to get lunch for his father, she turned her head toward the sliding glass doors then looked back at Jeremiah. "You know. I could leave Isaac a note to get you up before the sun tomorrow and take you out to see the sunrise."

The older man gave her a lopsided smirk.

She wagged her finger at him. "Only if it's something you'd like to do, not just to make Isaac get up extra early."

Jeremiah's face crinkled at her catching his motivation.

"Then maybe after I catch a sunset in the hot air balloon, we can have Isaac take you out for the sunset."

Before Jeremiah could indicate if he'd like to see either, Tanner's stride announced his interruption. "Are you suggesting Dad go in a hot air balloon?" His eyes, the same color as his father's, burned with incredulity.

She chuckled before winking at Jeremiah. "You don't think that's such a great idea?"

She had to give Tanner credit for being observant. He scanned both of them before the tension left his broad stiff shoulders. "No, but neither do you."

"That's correct. I simply asked if your father would like to get up extra early tomorrow to see the sunrise. I watched it from a hot air balloon early this morning, and it was spectacular."

"You won't find me in a hot air balloon. Too many things can go wrong." He faced his dad. "If you want, I can make sure Isaac gets you up tomorrow for the sunrise."

Observing Jeremiah and his son was a study in contradictions. Tanner was actually trying, but Jeremiah seemed to resent his son's control over him. As Jeremiah shook his head, she could see Tanner stiffen again. Was he irritated with his father's stubbornness or hurt that his dad didn't accept what he offered? She hadn't noticed such conflict with Brody.

Tanner turned back to her. "I guess not. Are you really planning to go again to see the sunset?"

"Absolutely. It's exhilarating to be up there with the birds. I'm looking forward to it. In fact, I already booked it for next week. It's fun."

His brows rose before he shook his head. "I have too much to do to take time for fun. In fact, I need to finish Dad's lunch." With that statement, he strode back into the kitchen.

She looked at Jeremiah. "I better see if he needs help."

As she rose, Jeremiah nodded his head much faster than he had last week, which pleased her. She walked to the archway and stopped to watch Tanner move about the kitchen as if he was as familiar with it as he was the stables. "I noticed you don't have a cook. Need any help?"

"No."

She continued to the island and sat on a stool. "Why don't you have a cook?" She couldn't imagine her father not having one.

He didn't turn to look at her. "Dad said we were plenty old enough to learn how to cook ourselves. So we just take turns."

"Is that why you and Brody switch off feeding your father lunch every day?"

He nodded, but didn't turn around as he finished getting the tray together.

"I can understand where your dad was coming from, making you all learn to cook. One of the best meals I ever had was one I made after running the rapids on the Colorado River. We all camped out afterward and fished. Cooking up my fresh caught rainbow trout and adding crushed berries to it from around the campsite made it one of the best meals I've ever had."

He turned at that. "Hot air balloons. Running the rapids? Are you an adrenaline junkie?"

"Hardly." She waved off the suggestion. "They were only level two rapids. The whole experience was more about being outside and living in nature."

A grunt that sounded very similar to his father's came from deep in his chest before he turned back and lifted the tray. Without another word, he left the kitchen, his boot heels striking the tile floor loudly.

She listened as he greeted his father cheerfully, explaining what was for lunch. As much as she didn't want to give Tanner any kudos, she appreciated that he always spoke to his dad as if his father hadn't had a stroke. It was one less habit she'd needed to address. Brody, on the other hand, didn't say much at all to his father.

While Tanner was in the den, she pulled out her laptop and added her notes on the morning's session. She paused to grab a protein bar from her bag. She had plans to go to dinner with her friend Lauren. They'd made reservations at a new place in Phoenix that was modeled after a

Medieval Court. She'd been to one of those in Vegas just the weekend before, but since Lauren rarely got a night off as the single mom of three kids, she had agreed to go.

Finishing her notes and her protein bar, she rose and threw the paper from it in the trash. She couldn't help but notice the empty steak packages and the broccoli stems. The Dunn boys not only ate well, but cooked well. They would be a catch for any single lady who wanted a cowboy. She couldn't imagine her brothers cooking their own meals. Now that she thought about it, except for an occasional steak on the grill, she wasn't sure they even knew how to use the stove. She pitied the women who fell in love with them, if there were such women.

Tanner's boot heels announced his return, and she moved back to the stool. She wasn't unaware that he thought she'd take any opportunity to spy on his operation. He hadn't figured out yet that she could care less.

"He only ate half."

She looked over the island at the tray Tanner set down and stifled a smile. "If that's half, then he did well."

He looked at her and scowled. "He used to eat three times this much."

"And he used to be out working the ranch all morning. He's not as physical as he used to be. Wait until I can get him moving more. Then his appetite will pick up."

Doubt filled his gaze, but he didn't say anything as he went about wrapping up what was left for the next day.

As much as Tanner didn't like talking to her, it was

clear to her that he knew his father far better than Brody, so he would just have to deal with it. "I need your advice."

"My advice?" He stopped what he was doing and gave her his undivided attention. "And here I thought you knew everything."

As annoyance filled her, she noticed the same twinkle in his eye that his father got. Wiseass. "Well I do, when it comes to what I want to know, but in this case, I need a little more information."

"Really." His left eyebrow rose, accentuating his sarcasm.

"Yes, really. I need to know what motivates your father."

He blinked before his brow lowered. "Why do you want to know what motivates Dad?"

Tanner was easier to read than his father. "You can stop thinking what you're thinking right now. I'm not looking for company secrets. Heck, I don't even know why our two families hate each other so much." Well, she did know it was because the Dunns were all about themselves and screw everyone else, but she didn't know the specifics.

"You don't know why our fathers hate each other?" His disbelief was clear as he stepped back from the island as if she'd given him cooties or something.

"No, I don't. My father said it was between him and Jeremiah. And since *I* respect my dad, I haven't pried."

His jaw clenched, making it easy to tell he was struggling not to say something. Obviously, he knew more than she did, but she didn't want to learn it from him. Not sure if he could keep his knowledge to himself, she returned to her question. "So can you tell me what motivates your dad? I need to find something that I can use to prod him in his therapy. Encouragement only goes so far."

Tanner remained silent, but he no longer looked at her, so hopefully he was considering her request. His profile showed he had his father's chin and nose, but his cheekbones must have come from his mom. Those and his hair, which was far darker than Brody's or Jeremiah's.

"Dad is motivated by something being done."

Relieved he was trying to help her, she tread carefully. "That's a little vague. Can you give me an example?"

"Projects. Any project that he sets to get done, he's motivated to finish, preferably in the same day. If he wants a new gate on the small corral, then he moves mountains to get it done."

She pondered that, trying to think how she could incorporate that in his therapy. "So he's motivated by short term goals. Is he ever motivated by a long-term goal?"

"You mean like a vacation next year?"

"Yes, exactly." That was something she could definitely relate to.

"No." Tanner shook his head and went back to packaging up his father's lunch. "Dad says thinking that far ahead just leads to disappointment."

Ouch, that was a sad outlook on life. Did Tanner subscribe to that belief as well? She dismissed the thought. This was about Jeremiah not Tanner, and it was hard to say if his father still felt that way. So many things changed after a stroke. "What about rewards?"

"Awards? No my dad wasn't into those, but Brody was for a time." He opened the refrigerator and set the containers inside.

"No, not awards, but rewards. You know, like if you get the room painted, you can take the weekend off?"

"Oh, that used to work well with Brody." He paused. "Still does, actually." His lips quirked up just slightly. "But not so much with my father or me."

She was beginning to wonder if she got to know Tanner better, she'd know Jeremiah better, but that could be playing with fire and would only work if Jeremiah's personality had not been affected by the stroke. "You're a lot like your father." She hadn't meant to voice her observation, but having said it, she watched for his reaction.

He took a deep breath. "Sometimes. We butt heads a lot, but I respect him. And he listens to me once in a while."

She was well aware that he hadn't said his father respected him. Then again, parents rarely thought that way. As children, even as the eldest, they were still children to them though she was pushing thirty. "Thank you. This was very helpful. I'm going to study a few methods now that I know what used to motivate your dad." She tapped on the keys of her laptop to add notes so she could check into different modalities.

"What do you mean 'used to'? Do you mean like what

Isaac said, that my father's personality might be changed in some way?"

Had Isaac told him that? It was better when a counselor talked to the family, and she was no counselor. "Yes, but that doesn't mean he *has* changed, which is why I need to know what has always motivated him."

He gave her a curt nod, then washed his hands and started to walk out of the kitchen.

Something in his walk told her he was escaping his own thoughts, and she wanted to reassure him. "Tanner?"

He stopped. "Yeah?"

"Your dad is going to get better and better."

His gaze drifted away from hers. "Yeah." Then he continued out.

She remained at the island as the front door closed. She couldn't help feeling for Tanner, even if he was a Dunn. He obviously loved his father and looked up to him. His father's health issue had been sudden, which must have caught him off guard. It was clear Tanner wanted everything the way it was before, but he was beginning to sense that it would never be the same. Did he realize he would probably never hand the reins of the ranch back to his father?

Her instinct said he didn't, and her eyes grew misty. If her father could see her now, he'd be furious. Luckily, he had no idea who her patient was, or that she sympathized with the son.

Closing her laptop, she walked back into the den where Jeremiah had fallen asleep in his recliner after lunch as he usually did. While asleep, he looked like any fifty-two-year-old man, except for the loose clothing.

She smiled. Jeremiah still wore his button-down shirts for her. That little sign made it clear that he needed her, even if he didn't realize it. Maybe she should dress up for him? Oh, now that might very well be a motivator. Would Tanner notice too? Scolding herself for thinking that, she quietly walked back into the kitchen and jotted down a new note.

CHAPTER 3

TANNER SLOWED Fury to a stop and read the email on his phone from the Town Council. "Shit. I don't have time for this."

"Don't have time for what?" Brody brought his horse closer. "I thought you said culling out the pregnant cows saved time."

Stuffing his phone in his jeans' pocket, he rubbed the back of his neck. "Not that. Keep separating them. Some are ready to start calving and with the monitors still down after the last storm, we're going to need a man on watch."

"So what don't you have time for?"

Sleep. That's what he didn't have time for lately. They needed to hire another cowhand or two, but that meant time, too. "It's the Town Council. They just emailed me asking a dozen questions. I'm going to have to ride in and answer them. They want them by close of business today."

Brody's brow lifted. "Today? They do know we're running a ranch, right?"

"Obviously not. They must think we're sitting on our thumbs just waiting to find out what our fate is." Movement in his peripheral vision had him turning. He raised his arm and pointed. "Nash! Better get that bull away. He's sneaking up on you."

Nash swore and turned his horse around.

Once he was sure his cowhand had the animal under control, he turned back to Brody. "I'll just make it short and sweet."

"Uh-uh. Since when is that going to satisfy the Town Council. You saw Dad's request. It was a flippin' twenty-two pages long."

Irritation flared. "I don't have time to write a damn book."

Brody held up both hands. "Hey, relax. I'm not suggesting that. What I suggest is that you compose it then replace me out here, and I'll add to it." He grinned. "You know I have a way with words."

That was true, whether it was a letter to a supplier or a woman just in town for a few days, his brother could change their mind. Brody's idea was sound, but it rankled. He should be able to handle it himself. He was the eldest. He was supposed to be taking over in twenty years. Then again, his father always said a good leader was one who knew how to tap into the strengths of those around him. "Fine. Finish getting the pregnant cows separated without letting the bulls and steers disrupt everything. I'll be out as soon as I finish the rough response."

"Great." Brody turned his horse and headed for the other side of the herd.

Tanner kicked Fury into a gallop and headed back to the house. Part of him wanted to just ignore the Town Council altogether, but he owed it to his father to give it his best shot. It wasn't as if he'd figured out any other way to keep their small ranch viable. None of this would be happening if Bill Hayden hadn't convinced the Town Council that they should turn the land adjacent to their northern border into conservation land even though his dad had already made an offer on it.

If that five-hundred-more acres was part of Rocky Road Ranch today, they'd be fine, not dancing to the Town Council's tune once again. At least Bill Hayden didn't sit on it anymore. His conservation land stunt had earned him enough popularity to gain a seat in the state legislature where he could screw up more lives.

As he galloped across the ranch, the all-too-familiar anger grew. He didn't want Rocky Road to turn into a dude ranch. But even as he gripped the reins, his mind spun in circles, trying to figure out another option.

Once near the barn, he slowed Fury and walked him inside, giving the horse a brief respite from the desert heat. Looping the reins over a hook in the stall, he checked that there was water before making a beeline for the house. It had to be after three already. If he'd been any farther west, he wouldn't have had phone service. That was another thing on his to-do list. Find some way to boost the signal. Maybe he'd put Brody on that too.

Opening the door to the house, two sensations hit him at once, the cool air from the air conditioning and the scent of vanilla, *her* scent. He slammed the door at the reminder that there was a Hayden under his very roof. It amazed him that he could forget that even for a few hours.

"Come on, Jeremiah. You need to at least try it." Amanda's voice was coaxing. "You don't really want mean old Tanner or the easily distracted Brody to feed you for the rest of your life, do you?"

No sounds followed, though a niggling hope had surfaced that there would be an answer.

"Me? Oh no, I'm not staying here the rest of your life to feed you. And no, Valeria isn't either."

The voice of the occupational therapist followed, and he walked in the opposite direction. Mean old Tanner? He wasn't mean. He was nice. He was one of the good guys, but he couldn't expect a Hayden to recognize that. True, he wasn't easy going. No, he was...he was serious. He had a lot going on, that's all.

But she was right about Brody. He was always being distracted by the next new thing. Actually, he was surprised his youngest brother was still at the ranch. He had no doubt the only reason Brody stayed was because Jackson was overseas.

Sitting down at the desk, he powered-up the desktop computer. Digging in his pocket for his keys, he unlocked the file drawer on the bottom right side of the large desk and pulled out the file on the dude ranch. Since his father had his stroke, he'd avoided it like last week's leftover gizzards, but it looked like he'd have to delve into it now. He pulled up the email on the desktop and read the attachment.

"Shit. How the hell am I supposed to know what kind of traffic will be added to Black Spur Road?" He continued reading the questions about everything from food service certificates to building permits to emergency evacuation protocols. "We're screwed."

He glanced at the five-inch-thick folder sitting on the desk. Could his father have all the answers in there? It wasn't like he could just go in the other room and ask him. Opening the folder, he found the original twenty-two-page request. Setting that aside, he discovered a site plan done of the property with new buildings added to it.

Leaning back in the leather chair, he studied the map. Why hadn't Dad shared this with him? Even as he asked the question, the answer came. Because he'd argued against the dude ranch since the moment the idea was introduced. A strange ache in his chest caught him off guard. It was a mixture of hurt, regret, and shame. He'd let Dad down.

He sat forward and placed the site plan to the left of the computer. There was no way in hell he would fail his father a second time. Re-reading the top question, he began rifling through the file for the answers he needed.

He spent the next hour and a half digging through the paperwork and answering the numerous questions. To his relief, most of the answers were there and anything he couldn't find, he talked around it. Hopefully, they would just ask clarifying questions on those. As he searched through the papers spread on the desk for the answer to the last question, quiet footsteps sounded down the hall. Glancing at the time on the computer, he froze. There was no way he'd get Brody in to finesse what he already had. He barely had time to finish it.

Frantic now to get it all completed in the ten minutes remaining, he stood and started piling documents in one corner. He'd seen the information on traffic estimates and road improvements somewhere. It was on letterhead of some sort.

"Hey, do you have a minute?"

He didn't need to look up because he knew it was Amanda and his frustration mounted. The last person he had time for right now was a Hayden. "No. I don't. If I don't find this damn estimate for this email in the next five minutes all my father's efforts will be for nothing."

"Oh, well let me help. What are you looking for?" Her shadow came over the papers.

He looked up, ready to yell at her to get out of the light, but her soft smile took the wind out of his anger. "It's a paper with letterhead that talks about road traffic and repair."

"Okay, I'll take this half of the desk and you take that half."

Part of him said to tell her to get out because he didn't want her to see everything his father planned, but the clock was ticking and he had no choice.

As she immediately started searching, the decision was taken from him.

Swallowing his panic, he fingered through a pile of papers interrupted by a map, which he threw to the side. He still needed to word the answer correctly and get the email off. Flipping over the top half of the pile, he started through the next half. It had to be—

"Is this it?"

He looked up to find her holding out a piece of letterhead from an engineering firm. He grabbed it and scanned it. "Yes!"

Sitting back down, he quickly put in the numbers the Town Council wanted, typed in a quick *sincerely* along with *Tanner Dunn on behalf of Jeremiah Dunn* and hit 'send.' He glanced at the clock. It was one minute until five. Collapsing back in the chair, he let out a breath.

"It looks like you're planning some improvements to Rocky Road." She held the site plan in her hands.

Jumping up, he pulled it from her. "Possible improvements."

She hooked her finger over her shoulder. "I sure hope your rocky driveway is one of them. Oh, is that what that paper was about?"

He held his arm out for her to leave the room. Taking the hint, she walked out ahead of him, and he locked the door behind him since he hadn't had a chance to lock everything back up in the file drawer. "You wanted to talk to me?"

She waited in the hall for him to finish with the door, but didn't move when he faced her. "Yes. It's about Jeremiah."

That she didn't smile when she said it had his gut tightening. "Is everything okay? Do you need more equipment?"

She waved off his questions. "No, I have everything I need. I just have a concern and a question, but it's a little delicate."

He'd been about to move toward the kitchen, but changed his mind. There was no need for Dad to overhear anything. "Then please continue."

"Could you tell me when your mother died?"

"What does that have to do with—" Her hand on his arm stopped his thoughts altogether.

"Please, don't get upset. I'm just gathering information, so I can best motivate your father." She dropped her hand.

His mother's death had almost killed his dad. "I don't see what this has to do with motivating my father."

"No, that's not...what I mean is...can you just answer the question first?"

"We never talk about Mom around Dad. I advise you not to as well."

"I understand."

She kept staring at him with her blue eyes, willing him to tell her what she wanted to know. It wasn't as if she couldn't find out in the town records. It was public information after all. "She died fifteen years ago of respiratory failure."

"Oh." Her eyes widened before she looked away. "I thought it was more recent. I'll need to think on this." She started to head down the hall.

He caught up to her and grasped her arm. "Wait a minute."

She halted.

He let go of her, regretting his action immediately. He knew better than to grab a woman. What the hell was wrong with him? He stifled an apology as she looked at him, her eyebrows raised in question. "Why did you want to know when my mother passed away?"

Instead of answering, she appeared to think about why she had asked. "Did they love each other?"

He jerked his head back at the insult. "Of course they did."

She smiled. "It's not always a given. My mother only wanted my father as a stepping stone in her ambition to be a Washington, DC wife."

He'd had many friends whose parents had divorced, but he'd never heard someone state the reason so baldly. A tinge of empathy for the Hayden offspring crept into his mind, but he stifled it. "Well, my mother and father loved each other."

"That's actually more concerning." Her brow knit together as her gaze drifted from his.

"Why?" He didn't want to admit it, but her opinion on his father mattered. As much as he hated the Haydens, he couldn't help but accept the expertise Amanda had in her job. He'd read her therapy plan, while looking up the technical terms on his computer, and she was very thorough. But more than that, she had a sincere compassion, something he hadn't seen at the hospital.

"The occupational therapist told Jeremiah that he couldn't expect his wife to wait on him hand and foot."

"What?" Outrage burned through him, and he took a step, ready to give the new therapist a piece of his mind.

Two hands against his chest stopped him cold, and he looked down to see Amanda's fingers splayed over his white shirt, her nail-polish-free nails blending in.

"Wait. She didn't mean anything by it. She didn't know your mom had passed. She's not from Four Peaks. Believe it or not, there's life beyond this town."

He moved his gaze from her hands to her face and found amusement twinkling in her eyes and her lips lifted in a smirk. He stepped back, not happy with the riot of emotions boiling inside him, including the way it felt to have her hands on his chest. "I know that." He sounded grumpy even to his own ears.

"It was your father's reaction to her statement that caught my attention."

"Why?" Concern cancelled out all other emotions. "What did he do?"

She squinched the right side of her face. "Um, it wasn't so much what he did, but how he looked. I wasn't sure if it was longing for something he'd lost or longing to be with his wife now. My concern is that it may be the latter."

He let out a relieved breath. "I can tell you that my father would not wish to be with my mother right now no matter how much he loved her. He's a fighter."

"I'm happy to hear that, but Tanner, you don't know what it's like to be unable to walk, talk, or simply feed yourself. It's not just humbling and humiliating. It can make you wish you no longer existed."

He scowled, not liking what she was saying about his father. Suddenly, he remembered that she had gone through something like it. "Is that how you felt?"

"Not all the time, but I admit there were days when I wished I had died. And my prognosis was far better than your father's."

This time sympathy for what she endured closed his throat. In high school, he hadn't thought about what it was like for her to be in a wheelchair when she came back to school. In fact, he was pretty sure he may have thought she deserved whatever happened because she was a Hayden. The thought did not sit well with him, especially knowing she'd wished she wasn't alive. But his dad couldn't be thinking that. He never gave up on anything. Still, worry niggled its way through his confidence in his father.

"Of course, I can't be sure yet." She shrugged. "I've only been with your dad a couple of weeks now and I'm still getting to know his nuances. Every expression and movement means something."

He swallowed hard, forcing his throat to work. "Do you think this is just a bad day type of thing for Dad?"

"I don't know." She shook her head. "I don't even know if I'm interpreting his look correctly. But if I see something of concern, I'll let you know. As his medical surrogate, you have that right."

"I would think my right comes from being his son."

Though he knew what she said was true, it pissed him off that just being a Dunn wasn't enough in the medical field.

Again, she gave him a soft smile. "I know. This is difficult for you and your whole family to navigate. You're doing fine."

At her kindness, his gut rebelled. She treated him as if he were a family member of another one of her patients, but he wasn't. He was a Dunn and she was a Hayden, and she needed to remember that. "I don't know why you would care. I'm a Dunn."

Her smile disappeared and her chin lifted. "Of course. How could I forget that fact when your rudeness makes it so obvious?" With a strong turn of her head, she spun on her heel and stalked down the hall.

He couldn't help smiling behind her back as she squeaked all the way into the kitchen, her sneakers making her irritation known. He lost his smile as he realized he'd been watching her ass. "Hell."

Turning back toward the study, he set the key in the lock when his phone buzzed. Pulling it from his pocket, he read the text.

YOU NEED TO TELL LULUBELL TO GO IN WITH THE REST OF THE PREGNANT COWS. SHE WON'T BUDGE FOR US.

He responded that he'd be right there and relocked the office. Damn heifer. Thought she was queen bee or something. All because he nursed her as a newborn when her mother died, she wouldn't do anything unless *he* told her to. Heading out of the house, he strode into the barn and prepared himself mentally to deal with the ribbing from his cowhands and his brother as he coaxed the lovesick animal to follow him into the fenced pasture.

Now, if only everyone else would follow him like that, his life would be easy street.

Five days later, Amanda was pretty sure she was right about Jeremiah. Even Isaac had noticed what he called "the gone" look, which was far different from the blank stare.

She patted Jeremiah's hand. "I'll be right back."

His expression didn't change as she walked out of the room.

Returning to the kitchen island where she left her laptop every day to take notes, she pulled up the hospital report again. There had been something in there. "Ah, here it is." Quickly she read it aloud. "An uncommon behavior that reveals strong flights away, anger, and depression." That was it! So why hadn't the hospital suggested continued counseling? Closing her laptop, she returned to Jeremiah, who greeted her with a smile and a pucker.

Her heart squeezed now that she understood. He didn't care about getting better because he didn't believe he would. They would have to get him some help right away, but maybe there was something she could do in the meantime.

"Okay, enough of that. You get an A for those two movements but an F for tongue exercises."

Jeremiah shrugged his shoulders, one raising more than the other, but not by much. "Brody was telling me about Maximus. Don't you want to improve so you can ride him again?"

Jeremiah's whole demeanor changed. His body stiffened and he shook his head.

"You don't? I thought you and Max were close."

The man's eyes narrowed and a sneer formed on his lips. It was an actual sneer, something she hadn't seen him do since she'd started.

At the sound of the front door closing and boots walking through the foyer, Jeremiah's face relaxed into his usual stare.

"Hey, Dad. I'm here to make you lunch!" Brody yelled from the kitchen even as they heard him open a cabinet and withdraw a plate.

This could be her chance. "I need to talk to Brody." Jeremiah didn't respond which was just as well because the person she really needed to talk to was Tanner. That man had become a ghost since they last spoke, in and out without a word. She wasn't sure if it was because she helped him, and he resented it or because she'd scared him about his father, and he didn't want to know anymore. Then again, it could just be that she was a Hayden.

Granted, she probably shouldn't have touched him, but she couldn't have him yelling at Valeria, the occupational therapist. She entered the kitchen to find Brody closing the refrigerator door.

His eyes widened when he noticed her standing there. "Oh, it's you. How's he doing?"

"I'm not sure. Is Tanner around?"

He nodded toward the door. "He's in the barn. Why?"

"I need to talk to him about your dad and his horse."

Brody's brows rose, but he refrained from asking any more questions and focused on preparing his father's meal.

She was fine with that. She thought it special that the brothers took turns feeding their father lunch. She was impressed by that, especially when she thought of her own brothers.

As she stepped outside, she hooked a right toward the horse barn, passing what she suspected was Brody's horse standing in the shade of the porch, content to munch on hay that had been set in a hay feeder on the side of the porch. It was a smart idea to have something at the house when a quick ride in was necessitated.

She continued to the stables, one of the many required structures on any cattle ranch. Her father even used half of his for his ATV fleet. Stepping into the shade of the wooden building, she was thankful for the slightly cooler temperature, though she doubted it was more than a couple degrees cooler than the hundred and eleven outside. She let her eyes adjust to the darker interior before heading in toward the noises coming from a stall at the end.

She'd almost reached it when Tanner stepped out and closed the door. Perfect. Just who she needed to see.

He took a double take when he spotted her. "What are you doing in here?"

At least he'd dropped the "hell" part of his question. "I want to bring your dad out here to see his horse. Where's Max?" She turned to the side to look down the row, curious what a horse named Maximus looked like.

"No."

She whipped back around. "What do you mean, no?"

He strode by her. "No. Surely you remember what that word means."

She followed him into the tack room. "Of course I know what it means, but what I don't understand is why you won't let your father visit with his own horse."

He pulled down a bucket and rifled around in a wooden box for something. "It's too dangerous. Max is a big horse. One wrong move and my dad could be crushed."

She crossed her arms, not a little insulted. She knew her way around horses. "He doesn't even have to go in the stall with Max. He just needs to see him. Maybe even give him a pat or a treat. It would be like a reward for something he's accomplished."

He walked by her again. "No. I told you, Dad doesn't work for rewards. If Dad can't walk or ride, then he doesn't need to see his horse."

Shocked at how unreasonable he was being, she stood frozen to the spot. Since when did he become a tyrant? She dropped her arms and followed him to a beautiful roan quarter horse, where he tied the bucket to the pommel. "That's a little cruel. I think seeing his horse could cheer him up."

Tanner finally faced her. "Cheer him up?" He shook his head at her as if she'd lost her mind. "I guarantee you that won't cheer him up. That would be like rubbing salt in the wound."

"What?" Now she was thoroughly confused. "Horses are used in therapy all the time."

"Strange horses. Not *his* horse. I know if it was me, it would be torture to see the horse I can't ride." He paused, a calculated look coming into his eyes. "When you were laid up, would you have wanted to see your favorite bike, skateboard, prom dress?"

Surprised by his reasoning, she didn't have any words.

"That's what I thought. So the answer is 'no'." He pulled the reins from the hook outside the stall, and walked his horse out into the sun before swinging himself up onto its back. He turned his mount to face her. "No horse." With those final words, he rode out of sight.

"Jerk." She fisted her hands. "What does he know about therapy?" He was just acting like a Dunn, all about himself. But her conscience reminded her that wasn't true. She loosened her fingers. Tanner, if anything, was incredibly worried about Jeremiah getting better, sparing no expense, ensuring the therapy plan was the right one, asking questions, and even panicking when he thought his father's work for ranch improvements would go down the drain.

A nicker came from a stall at the far end, interrupting her thoughts. Curious, she walked that way, surprised to see another horse in the barn as well. His stall had a metal name plate—Havoc. The Dunn boys certainly chose destructive names for their mounts. When she reached the final stall, she found Maximus, according to the small etched wooden sign, a pure black quarter horse, who upon seeing her, walked toward her.

She let the stallion sniff her until his nose nudged her shoulder. "Ah, have you been forgotten these days or is someone riding you?" She stroked Max's neck, his ears twitching as he listened to her. "Surely they are taking you out, maybe switching off?" Any good horse owner wouldn't let a beautiful animal like Max stand around inside the barn for weeks. She was learning more about the Dunns, and her gut told her they took care of their animals. After all, they were their livelihood.

Still...an idea started to form. Brody was in with his dad. She had her jeans and boots with her for barrel racing exhibition practice after her shift. "Max, I bet you wouldn't mind a little exercise today, would you?"

The horse lifted his head as if he thought that was an excellent idea.

She grinned. "Then it's settled. I'll be right back." Running out to her borrowed truck, she slipped into the backseat and quickly changed. She was still at work, but that was exactly what this was all about. She had to convince Tanner that his dad be allowed to see, maybe even pet his horse. Closing the truck door quietly, so Brody wouldn't come out to see what she was doing, she slipped back into the barn and quickly saddled Max. He was a little taller than her own horse, but she boosted herself into the saddle and followed the worn path west.

Tanner couldn't be too far. She'd heard Brody talking about moving the pregnant heifers together, so they would have them closer rather than farther away, in case any needed help with their calves. Even as she rode, memories of helping her dad and brothers during calving season flitted through her mind. She'd been young, maybe eleven the last time she'd been allowed to help. Then her mom left and she'd been regulated to the house as if she were too delicate for cattle ranching.

What her father didn't know was every time he was gone overnight or for a few days, her brothers welcomed her help, though it never seemed to be when the calves were coming. From the looks of the semi-covered area ahead, she'd guess that was where Tanner was. Dozens of pregnant cows gathered beneath the shade of what looked like tarps held up by metal poles. She was so busy trying to understand the set-up that she almost missed the lone horse standing next to the outside fence. Riding up to it, she shaded her eyes since in her hurry she'd forgotten her hat. There was no one around that she could see, but a distinctive moo came from further back in the shade.

Squinting into the darkened area, she could see nothing except a man on the ground with a cow. That couldn't be good.

Jumping off Max, she tied him to the same fence and quickly opened the gate wide enough to slip through, before closing it tight. Tanner was completely engrossed in the cow on its side in an individual pen beneath the tarping. Had there once been a metal roof?

It may have been a long time since she'd helped a cow calve, but it didn't take a genius to figure out help was needed. "What's wrong?"

Tanner looked up briefly then took a double take before the cow heaved, and he quickly pulled on the OB chains, keeping his attention on the cow. "She didn't dilate enough."

"What can I do?"

He glanced at her again, opened his mouth then closed it before turning back to the cow.

"I'm here, so I might as well help."

He jerked his head toward the corner of the pen. "I've got lube over there and a pump she kicked when I was getting the chains on."

Now that her eyes adjusted, she could see the bucket of solution, but didn't see the pump. Stepping around him, she moved slowly, not wanting to startle the cow. She found the pump in the next pen, which was unoccupied. Kneeling down on the ground, she reached under the railing and grabbed it. Getting up, she lifted the bucket with her other hand and returned to the cow's back end.

"Okay, but this isn't going to do much if we can't get her up."

"I know that, but I can't coax her and pull at the same time."

"Let me see what I can do." Putting the bucket down far from where it could be spilled, she moved to the front of the cow and squatted. "Hey, sweetie. I need you to get up, okay?" She stroked the cow's head. "Believe me, it's for your own good." Standing again, she walked to the back side of the cow as she lay on her side and pushed.

She got a moo for her efforts. "Really?" Getting down on her butt, she pressed her back against the cow, set her feet against the ground and pushed with her legs. Again, she got a complaint, but the cow rose onto her legs.

Quickly, she stood. "That's a good girl." Ducking under the rope that held the cow to the side rail, she grabbed the bucket and pump.

Tanner had risen with the cow, the calf's front feet now showing. "She's going to need a lot."

"Got it." Pulling the cow's tail out of the way, she pumped in a liberal amount of liquid.

On the cow's next heave, Tanner pulled, but the calf didn't move much. She pumped in more. Again a heave, and again the calf barely moved an inch. "Is the head in the canal?"

Tanner nodded as the cow heaved again and he pulled. She added more fluid, hoping they would have enough, hoping the cow had enough strength, and hoping the new calf would be alive when it came out.

For the next twenty minutes the three of them continued, the calf making slow progress, when finally the head popped through. Hope surged forth and tears stung her eyes.

"Just keep the tail back."

Not questioning Tanner, she stopped lubricating and in a few more minutes the rest of the calf fell into the hay with his help.

She let go and stepped out of the pen with the bucket and pump as Tanner expertly detached the OB chains, cut the umbilical cord, and untied the cow.

He stepped out as well and joined her. They both stood at the gate of the pen, watching as the cow began to lick the calf.

She tried to discern if the calf breathed by watching its stomach, but couldn't tell. After a few minutes of silence, the calf's nose lifted toward its mother's tongue.

Relief washed through her and she smiled, wiping her tears against the inside collar of her shirt.

"Are you crying?" Tanner's green gaze and furrowed brow made it clear he was bewildered by her behavior.

"They're happy tears. We helped that baby come into this world."

"It's a cow."

She wasn't about to let him know she hadn't seen a calf born in almost two decades. "It's a baby. Any new life is worth celebrating. And if we weren't here to help her, neither might be alive right now."

At that, he wiped the sweat from his brow with the

upper arm portion of his sleeve, the rest coated in birthing fluid. "Yeah. That is worth celebrating." He turned back to look at the cow, his profile softening.

It appeared there were many layers to Tanner Dunn. She finally returned her gaze to the calf, it's mom busy cleaning it up. Neither of them spoke. There was something so elementally natural about a mama cow and her baby. A peace she hadn't felt in a long time filled her.

"We better get washed up. This way."

Tanner's voice brought her back to reality. Her hands and sleeves were covered in guck. Almost his entire shirt was worse because he'd caught the calf as it came out.

Following him further beneath the cover, she saw a spigot and shower head.

He pointed to the tap. "You can wash up there."

Happy to get clean, she moved to the spigot and found a refill container of body wash. Grinning, she poured some in her hand before turning on the water. It was quite warm, as all water was in the summer in Four Peaks, but there was a chance it would get colder depending on how deep the well was and—the sound of more water had her turning. She stilled.

Tanner had taken off his shirt and now stood in front of the shower, rinsing his arms, neck, and chest. Water coursed down his torso between the fine dark hairs on his chest and over his undulating abdominal muscles before settling into his jeans. His arms were lifted, his biceps bulging as he wiped his face.

Heat formed low in her belly, catching her unawares and she sucked in a breath.

"Pass me the wash?"

Blinking, she grabbed the bottle and held it out.

He stopped rubbing his face and opened his eyes. "Thanks."

After he took the body wash, she quickly closed the spigot and walked back toward the pen, drying her hands on her jeans, but she couldn't resist looking back.

Tanner, bent forward, washed his hair with the body wash, the muscles in his back dancing with his movements. His shoulders were broad and his back narrowed at the waist just above his jean covered butt, which was rounded perfectly.

Her fingers tingled, and she snapped her head around to focus on the cuteness of the newborn, but all she could see in her mind was the water washing over Tanner's body. She *could not* be attracted to him. Simply could not. He was just the first man she'd seen naked from the waist up since being married to Claude. Her ex prided himself on going to the gym, but his pasty white skin and miniature body build was hardly cowboy strong.

Gripping the fence rail, she refused to look at Tanner again, even though she wanted to in the worst way. She really needed to get out more. This was proof it was time to start dating again, even if it was just for fun.

The dirt crunching beneath his boots told her he approached. He stopped next to her, but didn't face the cow. In her peripheral vision, she could see he'd put his hat back on and held his shirt in his hand. She couldn't just ignore him, so she turned.

"What the hell are you doing out here?" His scowl was back as was his favorite word.

Now if she could just stop staring at his chest and remember why she rode out in the first place.

CHAPTER 4

HE PULLED on his anger to tamp down the rush of desire that hit at the look in Amanda's eyes. She stared at his torso as if she wanted to lick him. Shit. He'd never had anyone look at him like that, at least that he could remember. Granted, it had been a good long while since he'd been with a woman. Why wasn't she with his dad? "Well?"

She finally lifted her gaze to his, and he caught his breath at the desire in the depths of her blue eyes. She blinked, taking a step back.

On second thought, he didn't want to know. Turning on his heel, he strode back toward the gate.

"Wait."

At her voice, he didn't hesitate, just kept walking. He needed to get as far away from her as possible.

A long loud moo, however, stop him in his tracks. Shit. If it wasn't one female then it was another. Changing direction, he headed for Lulubelle and the birthing enclosure he'd locked her in so he could help the new calf be born without his lovesick cow interfering. That heifer didn't care about anyone or anything else except her own needs.

"Tanner?"

At the moment, he'd take Lulubelle over Amanda Hayden in a heartbeat. Continuing to ignore Amanda, he unlocked the gate of the individual birthing enclosure and stepped back.

It must not be his lucky day because Lulubelle wasn't happy with him and instead of running out to join the other pregnant cows, she turned toward him, backing him into the fencing and pushing her head into his chest. He grabbed her chin to pull her face up just as she stuck out her tongue and licked.

"Ugh, not again." Turning her head to the side, he slipped out from between her and the fence and quickly headed back to the exit, not unaware of Amanda's laughter. Not knowing or caring if she followed, he slipped through the gate and closed it before he untied Fury, jumped on his back, and kicked him in the direction of the stables.

He was halfway there before his stomach growled, reminding him it was lunch time and Brody must be giving dad his lunch. That still didn't give Amanda the right to ride out on Dad's horse to the birthing enclosure. Then again, he doubted the calf would have made it without her. Seeing as how she'd helped with that, he wouldn't yell at her for taking Dad's horse, and call it even. He'd be damned if he'd be beholden to a Hayden for help.

Stopping at the stables, he jumped off and brought Fury inside for some well-deserved water. He heard the sound of horse's hooves approaching and made the mistake of turning to watch her ride in. Despite her years at college and whatever else she'd done since marrying her lawyer, she still sat a horse well. Not just well, but as if born to it, which he didn't doubt she was. What he hadn't expected was the spark of attraction that hit him in the gut like a one-ton bull ready to stud. "What the hell?"

Returning to Fury, he added some fresh oats for him and started for the other exit, seeing no reason to talk to her anymore. But when he passed by Maximus' stall, his irritation got the best of him and he stopped, turning to face her just as she jumped down from her mount. "Make sure you rub him down, give him plenty of water and extra hay. He wasn't supposed to go out today."

She smiled, as if happy to do all of those things. "Of course." She hugged the horse around the neck. "I'm very pleased to have met you, Maximus."

He shook his head and started out, when one of his ranch hands came out of a stall. "Ernesto, what are you doing back here?"

His man looked past him then gestured toward the stall.

This couldn't be good. Following Ernesto, he expected the man to show him a lame horse, but instead the man stopped and lifted his phone, pointing to it. "I gotta go."

Since Ernesto kept his voice low, he did as well. "Why? What's wrong?" He hoped the man wasn't sick.

"My mom. I just got a call from my wife. They rushed Mom to the hospital. They're not sure what's wrong, but they're running tests. I gotta go be with her."

The second the man said hospital, his insides froze. He'd rather go to hell then back to that place. "Of course." Now he would be down another man, but what could he do? "Go. Keep me updated."

The man scanned the stable as if checking that everything was in its place. "I know this isn't good for you. I'll be back as soon as I can. I promise."

He clapped the man on the shoulder. "Hey, I get it. I've been there, remember? You go take care of your mom. Don't worry about us."

"Thanks." Ernesto quickly strode out.

He stood there staring after the man, mentally trying to figure out how he could cover all that needed to be done with one less man when he was already short two. Maybe he'd have Brody put that ad online for another hand. He'd been in no hurry to vet another worker, but there was no way he'd make it through the next few weeks of calving season down two men and now Ernesto.

"That was very nice of you."

"What?" More surprised by how Amanda could get so close to him without hearing her boot heels on the stable floor than by the statement, he was caught off guard.

She pointed to the open stable doors. "You letting him leave for who knows how long when you're short staffed.

That had to be hard." She stood on tiptoe, her hand on his bare shoulder as she kissed his cheek.

He wasn't sure if it was her understanding of his situation or her vanilla scent that had him turning his head to capture her lips with his. Not that it mattered. Her lips were so damn soft. At the touch of her hand on his neck, he wrapped his arm around her. She opened her mouth, and he didn't decline the invitation.

As their tongues met, a crack of desire shot through his gut and he pulled her hard against him. She tasted of sweet tea and something more. Whatever it was, a craving started in his stomach as need began to build. He could feel himself growing hard, when a horse neighed and he remembered where he was and who he was. More importantly, who he was kissing.

He dropped his arm and pulled his mouth away abruptly, not even sure why the kiss started, but not happy about it.

Amanda immediately dropped her hand from around his neck, leaving a cool spot where she had touched him. "I better change and get back to your dad."

Before he could catch her reaction, she turned and walked purposefully from the stables.

He took off his hat and wiped the sweat from his brow, then placed it back on his head, the spot on his neck still feeling oddly cool. That wasn't happening again...ever. Suddenly uncomfortable, he scanned the building to make sure no one had seen him act like an idiot. Luckily, the only one staring at him was Fury. "What? Eat your oats."

The horse didn't do as he was told, which was hardly a surprise. Ignoring Fury, he headed for the exit. What the hell had he been thinking to kiss a Hayden? So what if she rode well, was attractive and soft, and smelled good. There were plenty of women out there like that. What he needed was a night out in town. But that wasn't about to happen. There was a reason he hadn't been out at night since his dad's stroke and that reason hadn't changed. In fact, now he was in worse straits than before.

Part of him wished Jackson would come home, but he always wished that. His brother's deployment caused a cloud over him that just never went away. There was always a niggling worry. Dad would tell him he coddled everyone, but his father wasn't there when Devlin fell.

He halted even as he reached for the door to the house. Instead of opening it, he placed his palm flat against it and took two deep breaths, counting to ten both times. Then he turned around and scanned the ranch from the front porch. The habit was the only way he kept from going down the dark tunnel of guilt that opened up every time Devlin entered his head.

From where he stood, most of the ranch was west of him with the driveway to the east. It was still theirs. He could be proud of that and that his father was home and getting the best care. His men were well-trained and safe. He still had control. He just had to focus on the next step, which was having Brody place the ad. Maybe he should let Brody vet any responses down to his favorite three. Even as the idea hit him, some of his tension left. Though Brody had no interest in taking the reins one day, it would still be good experience for him.

Turning back toward the door, he opened it, and strode in. Brody was putting the dirty dishes in the dishwasher as he entered the kitchen. "Did Dad eat everything?"

His brother shook his head. "No. But he ate half. I ate the other half. Another day and those leftovers would be rotten. Didn't think we needed to throw out good food."

"Good." Of course, that meant he'd have to make his own lunch. "Remember how you keep hounding me about hiring more men?"

Brody halted, the dish in his hand hovering over the top rack. "You going to?"

He walked to the fridge and pulled out a water bottle. "*You're* going to."

Brody's eyes widened. "Seriously?"

"Mostly." He pushed out a stool, opened the bottle, and took a gulp before sitting. "Go ahead and send out the ad you wanted to on that website. You get it narrowed down to three and I'll talk to them. Then we can decide who's best."

"Why now?" Brody added the dish and closed the dishwasher then washed his hands.

"Ernesto just left. His mom was rushed to the hospital."

"Well, flippin' A." Brody dried his hands with the towel. "It's like it's a pandemic. Is she going to be okay?"

"He doesn't know." Even as he said the words, the chilled feeling he got when he rode to the hospital with his dad skittered up his spine. "He says they're doing tests."

"That sucks."

Yeah, it did, for Ernesto and them. "So you think you can get that ad up tonight?"

"Sure thing." His brother gave him a wise smile. "Unless you'd like me to do it now, and you head back out to the pond."

The pond was a polite way of saying mud hole, which it only was when the monsoons came through. "No, tonight will do. I have to eat and get back out to the birthing pen to check on the new calf. Almost lost it."

"Was it stuck?"

"Yeah. She didn't dilate enough. I wish we had only experienced mothers, but there's always first-time ones to look out for."

Brody's sly smile was back as he motioned with his water bottle. "That why you're prancing around without a shirt? And here I thought it was to impress Miss Hayden."

The comment struck far too close, and he scowled. "Wiseass. Get back to work. I have lunch to make." He stood, pushing the stool back at the same time.

"I'm going." Brody held his hands up as if being robbed. "Don't shoot me over it."

He ignored his brother as he moved to the fridge, Brody hustling out of the kitchen. He had the roast beef, tomato, and mayo out by the time the front door closed. As he made his sandwich, he mentally calculated the budget in his head. He could hire two men if he had to, but one would have to be less experienced. That could be good or bad, depending.

He tried to stay focused on his lunch and his responsibilities, but Amanda's voice in the den kept distracting him.

"Come on, Jeremiah. You don't really want Brody feeding you for the rest of your life, do you?"

Her laugh followed. No surprise there. His father was probably being a wiseass. Brody was like him in so many ways.

"Very well. I was going to bring you Mrs. Silva's famous Cake Batter ice cream tomorrow, but if you can't eat it, there's no reason to bring it."

He shook his head even as he chewed. That wasn't going to work. His dad could never be bribed. He'd tried far too many times as a teen.

"Just think, if you master using a spoon, you can check off one utensil from your list of skills to master. But if you want to give up before the first one is even attem—oh."

He grinned. Now that was how to rile up his dad. Tell him he was a quitter and watch things happen. A soft pang hit his heart as a memory of his mother using that very tactic filled his head. She hadn't used it often, but that and telling his dad she'd hire someone who could take care of something would jolt his father into action faster than a bronco bucked off its rider.

Finishing his lunch, he set the dishes in the sink and headed to his room to grab a shirt. The last thing he needed was a sunburn. Grabbing a white and tan checked button-down that had seen better days, he buttoned it as he strode through the house, intent on getting back out to the new calf. If she wasn't nursing, he'd have to play mother, like he had with Lulubelle. He slowed his step. If that was the case, he'd put Brody on calf duty tomorrow. The last thing he needed was another lovesick heifer.

Walking into the entry, he grabbed up his hat and reached for the door.

"Tanner?"

Her voice was barely a whisper and still it sent a shiver through him. Turning, he was surprised to find that she looked as if she'd just seen a ghost, her face paler than usual and her eyes wide.

Immediately, every muscle tensed. "Yes. Is something wrong with my dad?"

She gave a short nod.

Hell. There was no one in the house, so they couldn't talk outside and leave his dad alone.

He pointed down the hall, and she started that way. As he followed, he forced himself not to look at her ass. Instead, he focused on her blonde ponytail. Her hair was very straight and fine. Most of it was white blonde but there were golden strands mixed in.

When she stopped, he did too, careful to keep at least four feet away, though he'd prefer four fields away. He kept his voice low. "What's wrong?"

"I just discovered your father can talk."

"What? That's great." The joy that rifled through him had him forgetting his volume and she pushed her finger against his lips. He froze, ignoring the urge to suck her finger into his mouth.

As if just realizing what she did, she dropped her hand. "Shh."

Why would the fact his father could talk have to be kept quiet? "I don't understand what the problem is."

She crossed her arms even as her brow furrowed. "Because of how I discovered it."

He didn't care how as long as it was true, but to humor her he asked the expected question. "How did you discover it?"

She leaned in. "He was talking to your mother."

His heart hiccupped at that. "My mother?"

"Yes. Did he do that before the stroke?" Her gaze was so hopeful, he didn't want to crush it.

But he shook his head. "Not that I know of. Dad never told me he spoke to Mom, and I never heard him. But I can ask Brody."

Amanda's look turned pensive. "That means it's a new behavior."

He didn't care if it was new. His father could talk! "But he's talking. That's a good thing, right?"

She met his gaze. "It's not clear. His words are formed, but barely. It's more like garbled mumbling, but he is vocalizing."

That sounded good to him. "To me that's excellent progress." If his father could talk, then he could ask him questions, get advice. Amanda still didn't seem to share his optimism, and it pissed him off. Did she have an ulterior motive? "What is it? Why aren't you thrilled that my father is talking?"

She uncrossed her arms and leaned against the hallway wall. "It was the way he did it. He was staring at something I couldn't see and having a complete conversation."

Even as she said the words, a chill raced up his spine. "Are you saying he's talking to my mother's ghost?"

"No, of course not. At least not a real ghost. But he sees her, even in his own mind and that worries me. It's another behavior that points toward suicidal thoughts."

A wave of anger hit him hard, and he clenched his fists. "My father is not suicidal."

Her blue gaze studied him like he was some scientific experiment she needed to figure out. "I didn't say he was, but I have concerns about his mental state."

"Well, you should. You said yourself that the stroke affected his brain."

"Yes, but in the sense of physical modalities and possibly his personality, not in his emotional state." She took a deep breath and stood straight, facing him head on. "You need to hire a psychologist. Even if it's just—"

"A what? You mean a shrink?" His brows lowered and his jaw tightened. "Dad is not mentally ill. He's dealing with his limitations. I get that. I'm sure it frustrates the hell out of him. He may be talking to my mom because he doesn't feel comfortable revealing his feelings to us. That's understandable. He still deserves to have his privacy, at least in this. His every move involves someone taking care of him, even bathing him. That would certainly piss me off." Now that he really thought about it, how little privacy Dad actually had made himself uncomfortable.

"Tanner, just give it some thought. What harm can it do?"

"A hell of a lot if he knows he's talking to a shrink. If he's fine, he'd never forgive me."

Her gaze turned cold. "Then that's just a risk you're going to have to take." Without another word, she brushed by him and started back down the hall.

He turned. "I don't have to do anything. I'm the one in charge, not you." Even as the words left his mouth, he grimaced. He sounded like a two year old.

She didn't turn around, but she threw her hand up, making it clear she was done talking to him.

He stalked after her, planning to continue the conversation, but she had packed up her fancy laptop and was heading out the door. "Wait, where are you going?"

"You're the one in charge, so take charge. He's all yours. I'm so done for the day." She opened the door.

"You can't. I'm paying you for the whole day."

She slammed the door shut in his face.

What the —a sound from the other room had him halting. Listening, he heard it again. It wasn't a creak. It was more like a squeak. Worry wormed its way through his mind, and he quickly headed to the den. Fearing his dad was trying to get out of his recliner on his own, he made it there in seconds.

Dad was right where he was supposed to be, in his recliner taking his afternoon nap. Relief washed through him even as he scanned the room for where the sound could have come from, but nothing made sense. Isaac was probably out on the back porch until his lunch break was over, so the room was empty except for his dad. Even the television was off.

Could Dad have moved and caused the recliner to squeak? He stepped into the room carefully, so as not to wake him. The tile beneath his feet didn't creak, but his cowboy boots could make a lot of noise. As he stepped closer, he could see his dad's lips moving. Maybe he snored and that was what made the sound.

Drawing closer, he could see his dad wasn't snoring. He was talking, but so softly and garbled that he couldn't make out what was being said. As he stood there listening, the sound happened again, but this time he could tell it wasn't a squeak, so much as a whistle.

They had a dog when he was younger who used to come when his dad whistled. Maybe Dad was dreaming about the past. Back then, the ranch was thriving, Mom and Devlin were alive, and they were happy. Even as his memory filled in the pieces, the joy of the time gave way to bitterness. How far they were from those happy times.

Quietly, he retreated back to the kitchen, wishing his father pleasant dreams, before the struggles, the betrayal, and the death. Life would never be like that again. Hell, he wasn't even thirty-one yet, and all he had to look forward to was survival? The thought had his mouth going dry and he grabbed another water from the fridge. Opening it, he took three full gulps, emptying half of it. He'd been so busy with Dad and the ranch, the daily tasks and concerns, he'd not thought about what happened beyond the next day.

He moved to the family room to sit on the couch, setting the bottle on the end table. Staring out the sliding doors opposite him, he frowned at the mountains in the distance. He'd always known Rocky Road would be his one day. Maybe when his dad was in his seventies. He'd been excited by that prospect. Now, it felt like a monsoon storm ripping through him, taking out chunks of him as he sought to hold on. What the hell had happened?

Amanda rolled her eyes at Jeremiah. "I'm not falling for that trick. I know for a fact you aren't tired. In fact, Isaac told me you overslept this morning."

Jeremiah shrugged, his shoulders unequal still, which concerned her. He should be progressing more, but he spent all his time goofing off. It had already been four weeks, and he continued to be stubborn about what he would and wouldn't do.

"Very well. If you aren't going to try to improve, then there's no reason for me to keep coming. I'll just tell Tanner he doesn't need me anymore." That would certainly make things easier for her after that kiss they shared. What had she been thinking? She covered the squeeze ball with her hand and started to pull it off the table, when Jeremiah grabbed her wrist.

"Nah!"

Part of her jumped with glee that she got him to speak in front of her, but his grip was far too tight to be happy. "Why not?"

He shrugged again, not looking at her, but didn't let go.

"If you want me to stay for some reason, you'd best be telling me why. I don't see why Tanner should pay me when I can't help you."

"Hep. Tanna. Stay."

"So you want me to stay, so you can help Tanner?"

Jeremiah thrust her arm away from him and spat at the floor.

Rubbing her wrist, she frowned, thoroughly confused. Could Tanner's dad really dislike him that much? She'd seen their relationship was contentious, though Tanner's love for his dad was painfully clear. "So you don't want to help Tanner?"

Jeremiah scowled before he slammed his good fist down on the table. "Kent!"

She jumped, surprised by the outburst since she hadn't seen Jeremiah mad since she started, but anger could be good. If she understood, the man felt that he couldn't be of any help. "Not now. You can't help until you gain your strength and coordination back. Then you can—"

"Kent!" He slammed his fist down again.

"Can't or won't?"

Jeremiah whipped his arm back into his lap and scowled at it, his lips stubbornly closed.

She understood the frustration more than he knew. At fifty-two, the once robust man was barely strong enough to lift a spoon and his body and mouth wouldn't work like he wanted them to. It had been demoralizing for herself as a teenager, but for a man of his age, a patriarch of a family, the head of a business, it had to be devastating. The more he acted out, the more she grew convinced he needed psychological help beyond her rudimentary understanding.

Somehow, she had to get Tanner to agree to hiring that help. That might mean forcing him to understand that his father would never be what he once was, or worse, admitting her own weakness. She didn't look forward to that conversation. Glancing at the clock, she realized she didn't have much time to prepare for it. Tanner would be in to make his dad's lunch soon. She'd avoided him for the last week when he served his father lunch, slipping out of the room to eat herself.

Their kiss had been a surprise that had her blood singing right down to her toes. That shouldn't be, not when he was a Dunn. She'd gone out dancing last weekend with girlfriends, hoping her reaction to Tanner's kiss was just her lack of time spent with men, or rather cowboys, to be specific. Unfortunately, the cowboys she danced with did nothing for her, and when one particularly bold fellow had moved in for a kiss, she had quickly turned away.

It had taken everything she had to tell Tanner about his dad talking to his mom. She'd been so thrilled when she walked in to hear Jeremiah talking, but when she moved close enough to hear him, her worry grew. However, when she'd stepped in front of Jeremiah and he kept looking at the empty space to her right, she knew something was very wrong. To have Tanner be so stubborn as to deny his father help because he refused to believe what a stroke could do to someone's mental state had just been too much.

She'd gone straight home and called LaReina in case Tanner called to complain, but he never did. Maybe he realized he was wrong and instead of avoiding him, she should have been talking to him? Maybe he was ready to listen. She didn't actually believe that, but she couldn't discount it as a possibility.

In the meantime, she had to try again to motivate Jeremiah. "Okay, so you're pissed. I get it. The least you can do is work on the words so you can make your anger heard and understood."

He didn't look at her, but his brow relaxed as did his mouth.

"I mean, if you're going to swear at someone, the least you can do is get the words right."

Jeremiah looked at her. "Shut."

She should have known he'd be happy to work on swear words. Pretending she had no idea what he meant, she rose. "You want me to shut the bedroom door?"

His scowl was back. "Shut." He shook his head.

"Remember those mouth exercises I've been teaching you?"

He lifted his good hand and pretended to yawn.

"Very funny. If you practiced them, you could swear right now like an angry trucker at a skunk in his cab."

Jeremiah frowned at her like she'd lost her mind.

"Never mind. Just focus. You already have the "sh" and "t" sound, so you only have to work on the short "i" sound."

The sound of the front door opening, told her she had an even harder discussion to look forward to in the adjoining room. "I'm going to let you practice while I talk to Tanner."

Jeremiah grinned and stuck out his tongue and wiggled it.

"Really? That's not the exercise for the short "i" sound. Now if you practice that one you can swear at Tanner."

The man's eyes lit with glee as he started to practice.

Now why did that motivate him? Was he that resentful of his son? She walked into the kitchen expecting Tanner but found Brody instead. "I thought it's Tanner's turn today?"

Brody took leftovers out from the fridge and popped open the container. "He called. He's running late. He had to go into town to meet with some of the Town Council members. Some planning committee or board or something. He should be here soon, but he didn't want dad to starve."

As Brody continued getting out a plate and silverware, she moved to the counter where her laptop was. Now, she'd have to wait until he arrived home. He'd probably be in a terrible mood like he was last time he had to do something for them. Rocky Road Ranch was obviously planning some kind of expansion or change, but it wasn't her place to find out what. The last thing she wanted was information about the ranch she would have to hide from her father.

Maybe she should wait until the day after tomorrow. The only time she saw him was when he had lunch duty. But she hated to wait much longer. She'd at least like a psych evaluation done.

"So how's Dad doing?"

She looked up from her laptop notes. Not sure what Tanner had told his brother, she kept things vague. "He's making progress, but only on what he wants to do."

"Yup, sounds like Dad."

She had to ask. "Was he always a jokester?"

Brody froze just as he opened the microwave. "What do you mean?"

She didn't know the youngest Dunn that well, but even she could see he'd grown a bit paler. "I mean, making faces, being a wiseass, that kind of thing."

"He was." Brody pulled the warm meal out and set it on the tray for his father, not looking at her. "Before Mom died." He turned with the tray and strode into the den. "Lunch time, Dad."

She stared at the empty archway to the den. It was another connection to the late Mrs. Dunn. Something definitely didn't feel right. Maybe it was the stroke that changed Jeremiah's personality. That could be, but her gut was telling her it was something more serious, and they needed to address it. It also made it clear that the only way she could be sure, or somewhat sure, to get through to Tanner was to tell him her own story. She'd mentioned it, but hadn't given him the embarrassing details.

Closing her laptop, she stared at it a minute. Should she tell Tanner about the joking, or had he already noticed? Not sure, she pulled her satchel over and opened it, digging out her protein bar. It was not nearly as appetizing as the warmed-up lasagna Brody had on the tray for his father. She had to wonder if he'd cook for his wife one day.

Just as she unwrapped the bar, she heard a truck pull into the front. Immediately her hunger dispersed. It had to be Tanner, and they had to talk. Now.

Hopping off the stool, she strode to the front door, determined to get the conversation done and over with in private. She stepped outside and halted in her tracks.

Tanner strode toward her in a suit and tie, clean shaven and looking good enough to be on a billboard for men's clothing. Holy shit, did he clean up nice! She hadn't realized exactly how broad his shoulders really were.

He approached her. "Brody get my message?"

She nodded, her throat tight at the sight of him.

He looked at her quizzically. "Is he in with Dad?"

She swallowed hard. "Yes." The word came out gruff.

"Good. I'm going to go change and head out to the north pasture then."

She nodded, then found her voice. "No, wait."

He had already brushed by her but came back. "What?"

As much as her stomach felt like the wave action in a

one-person swimming spa, she had to tell him now. "We need to talk about getting your father some additional help."

He raised one eyebrow. "Another person?"

She could feel the perspiration trickling between her breasts despite the fact they stood in the shade of the front porch, where it had to be only a hundred and five. "Yes. Your dad spoke to me today."

The tension left him, and he leaned his handsome self against the porch post. "That's a relief. What did he say?"

"He said he can't help you with the ranch." Though she knew it was a long shot, she hoped that that, in itself, would convince Tanner of the need for a psychologist.

Instead of being concerned, he grinned. "That sounds like Dad. Stubborn as the day is old."

Really? It was far more than that. "Actually, he's in there right now doing one of his mouth exercises so he can swear at you."

Tanner chuckled as he nodded. "It sounds like my old dad is back."

Despite the fact he was honestly thrilled with her news, she had to burst his bubble. "Exactly. Your 'old' dad is back. The one before your mom died."

That got his attention. He straightened. "What do you mean? What do you know about how dad was when mom was alive."

She shrugged, pretending a nonchalance she didn't feel. "Just that he was a jokester and that disappeared when he became a widower, only to resurface after his stroke. That could be because the stroke affected that part of his brain, or..." she hated telling families that their loved one wished he or she was dead.

"Or what?" He took a step toward her, towering over her as if daring her to say what was on her mind.

Little did he know that tactic never worked with her. Growing up with four brothers, there hadn't been a dare she didn't take, usually proving to them she was right. "Or he's reverted back to the happiest time of his life because living as he is now is impossible to accept. To be frank, your father would rather be dead."

His jaw clenched and his neck muscles stood out against the white color of his shirt before he spoke. "You have no idea what my father thinks."

She walked over to the bench set against the adobe wall and sat, not wanting to have Brody overhear her if he opened the door. "You're wrong. I do know what he could be thinking." She paused, staring at the dirt of the desert front yard. It was hard telling someone who cared about her what happened. It was almost impossible telling someone who didn't want to hear her or care. "I know because I thought that as well. In fact, I was so convinced that I could never be myself again, never achieve my dreams of being a champion barrel horse racer, never graduate high school and go to college...never even speak normally that I attempted to take my own life."

He turned toward her but he didn't say anything.

She continued. "When you are in a hospital for as long as I was, you get to know the routines, what dinner will be on Tuesday, when the nurses change shift, where they keep the drugs when handing them out. What I failed to recognize in my messed-up mind was that since I was in the hospital, my condition would easily be noticed. One minute I had drifted into pure oblivion, and the next I woke with a sore throat and felt like gagging. They had pumped my stomach."

"I didn't know." His voice was deep and low.

She clasped her hands, feeling as guilty and ashamed as she had at that moment, but what she also felt then, anger, was gone. Instead, she was grateful. "No one knew, except my dad, and of course he couldn't let it be known publicly since he was a state legislator." The old bitterness crept into her voice. "Just like no one ever knew why I was gone from school for so long and came back in a wheelchair. We were all told to keep it to ourselves."

She looked up at him to find his gaze sympathetic, and she couldn't stop herself. "It was just encephalitis that was so bad I went into a coma. It wasn't like I had a venereal disease or something, but with all the hush-hush about it, I felt guilty as if I'd done something wrong. Shit, I may very well have gotten it from a mosquito bite. But no, it was a big secret, and now I don't care if anyone knows."

His brows furrowed. "That's nothing to be ashamed of."

"Right?" Even as she said the word, she realized she'd gone off track. She rose, to bring herself back in line with her point. "The only reason I tell you this is that when you are in a condition like your father is, feeling like you're a waste of space is not uncommon. I know you don't want to hire anyone, but at least let me order a psych-evaluation. Maybe I'm wrong. I don't pretend to be a psychologist. But isn't it better to know either way?"

He stared at her a long time without saying a word. Then he lifted his black cowboy hat and wiped his forehead with a white handkerchief, before finally speaking. "Let me think about it."

At least it wasn't a definite no. "Of course. I apologize if I shared too much." She reached for the door, but he caught her arm.

"I'm sorry you felt that way."

She swallowed at the look in his eyes as if he'd like to take the memory from her. "Thank you."

He let go then, and she opened the door, ducking inside. It wasn't until she reached the kitchen that it hit her. If the Dunns were all about themselves, then why would Tanner care about what she'd gone through?

Brody walked in with the tray of leftover lasagna. "Didn't you say his appetite should be improving?" He sounded accusatory as he set the tray on the counter with barely a fourth of the lasagna gone.

She cringed, the lack of appetite was not a good sign. "Give it time. He's only been home a month."

"How long does he need?"

Brody's frustration was palpable. Yet it was nothing compared to what Jeremiah felt. "As long as it takes."

He hmphed. "Talk about job security."

Before she could respond, he stormed out the door, leaving the tray where it was.

She understood the man's frustration. It often happened with family members, and she was often the brunt of the family's feelings, but it all turned around eventually.

Then why did she feel as if she were failing... miserably?

CHAPTER 5

TANNER SAT on Fury watching the last rays of the sun turn from orange to pink as it set between two of the four peaks for which the town was known. Amanda's revelations earlier in the day had him thinking as much about her as about his father. Though he'd never wished for death himself, he had wished with all his young heart that it had been he who fell from the hayloft that summer instead of Devlin, but that was due to guilt, not to giving up.

Could Dad, the man who whipped his butt when he got drunk while underage, and who commanded the ranch hands with authority, really prefer to leave them all and be with Mom? It was a sobering thought. If, as a young teenager, unable to see a future caused Amanda to think death was preferable, what was it like for his dad, past his prime with the love of his life already gone? Amanda had recovered completely from what he could see, but Dad did not have the same prognosis, not according to the paperwork.

He tried to imagine how it would feel, not being able to ride, take pride in the ranch, or even enjoy a well-cooked meal, which Dad so often did. Did he know he'd never be one hundred percent? No one could even say what he would be able to do eventually. Was feeding himself the most he could look forward to? Even at the thought, Tanner could see how bleak life could look.

The sound of a horse's hooves coming closer gave him a heads-up he'd soon have company.

Brody brought Chaos to a stop next to him. "That last patch of fence is mended. Does that mean we can wait on the birthing enclosure repairs until after the calves have been born? I doubt the heifers will want us putting a new roof up while they're around."

He looked at his brother. "Yes, we'll wait. We need every one of those calves to make it. I don't want anything to jeopardize that."

His brother chuckled. "And you certainly don't want Lulabelle mad at you."

"That's not what concerns me. It's ending up with another Lulabelle. If one of those mom's doesn't make it, you'll get nanny duty this time."

"I don't think so, bro. I'm only staying until Jackson gets home, then Dad won't need me anymore. If I end up Mommy to one of those calves, you'll just end up taking over anyway."

His stomach knotted, just as it always did when his youngest brother talked about leaving the ranch. When

Brody was younger, it was to be a trick rider, then later it was a pilot, but more recently, it was to become a game ranger. The fact that Brody had already taken all the courses proved how serious he was about it. He'd never been the studying type, just getting by with his grades. Of all of them, he'd been the most easy-going and the one that caught the ladies' attention.

"You're brooding again. What's the problem now?"

Brody shook his head. "Still sure you want to run this place?"

"Hell yeah." It's what their father had always planned, but he wasn't quite ready to fly solo yet. "I love this ranch. Just look at it." He faced forward again, the sun having gone down, but the pinks in the sky spread further, turning purple in places.

"Yeah, I love it too. It's just that I need a change, something different. There's no saying I won't be back to mess up your perfectly run operation."

He raised his eyebrow, knowing that would be exactly what Brody would do. Brody wanted change, and he liked things just the way they were. But if the Town Council was happy with all his assurances today, there'd be a big change. He faced him again. "You know, running a dude ranch is different from running a cattle ranch."

"I wouldn't know, nor do I want to. Nothing against the way you're running the ranch, big brother, but Jackson got his chance to do what he needed to do. The way I look at it, it's my turn."

Yeah, it probably was, but he still didn't like it. He set his gaze back on the sunset, which was more like twilight now. "We'd better get in and get dinner started." He tapped Fury on the shoulder. "Let's go home, boy."

Brody turned with him. "You can make whatever you want. I'm going out tonight, remember?"

Did he? No. "That's right. Okay, so it will be just Dad and me."

"You know, you need to get out once in a while, too."

At his brother's suggestion, he laughed. Instead of answering such an absurd comment, he kicked Fury into a gallop and headed for home.

His brother kept up with him, the ranch hands having long headed out, so it was just the two of them on the ride to the barn. They each took care of their own mounts in silence. He'd take Maximus out tomorrow. Dad's horse was in much better shape than Dad. Brody would ride Havoc, Jackson's horse.

"I'm going in to shower." Brody slapped his hand on the stall door. "Don't wait up for me."

He glanced over his shoulder. Brody was grinning from ear-to-ear. "Get out of here."

"Don't have to tell me twice."

Tanner turned back to Fury and finished brushing him down, his younger brother's whistling grating on his nerves until the front door closed and silence reigned once again. He never remembered being that young. At twenty-seven, he'd been too busy proving to his dad that he could handle the ranch. He paused in the brushing. Hell, he'd been doing that since he was nine, maybe ten. Shaking his head at himself, he finished up and patted Fury. "See you tomorrow."

Heading out of the stables, he couldn't help thinking that with Brody gone, tonight would be the perfect time to talk with Dad. The only problems he could foresee with that plan were that he didn't want to, and his dad couldn't talk.

He hesitated as he reached the house. Amanda said his dad could talk somewhat. That in itself had him opening the door and striding in, his step a bit lighter. If Dad could talk, he could weigh in on the Town Council meeting, maybe even give him some advice on prioritizing the many repairs that were still needed after the monsoons that hit last year.

Dropping his hat on the front entry table, he entered the kitchen and pulled a water bottle out of the fridge. He'd just unscrewed the cap and lifted it to his lips when Amanda's footsteps sounded on the floor before she stepped into the kitchen.

"Another water bottle? You do know you left one by the sink over there earlier, right?"

He twisted around to see he had. "I'm sure there are at least five others about the house. It's not as if it goes bad." He picked up the half empty water bottle and set it in the fridge to cool down again. He hated warm water.

"True." She zipped up her satchel. "I'm out of here. Heading into Phoenix for a Diamondbacks game. I try to take one in every year. You know, support the home team and all that." She flung her satchel over her shoulder. "Isaac just brought your dad in for a shower. I'll see you tomorrow."

With that she headed for the entry way.

"Wait." The word was out of his mouth before he even knew what he wanted to say.

She stopped, her brows lowering in concern. "What is it?"

He shook his head as much as much at himself as at her. "Nothing important. Just wanted to know how Dad did this afternoon."

"Pretty much the same. But I'll keep trying."

"Thanks. I appreciate that."

She studied him for a moment then gave a quick nod. "See you later."

Though he knew he shouldn't, he couldn't help watching her walk out the door. Her revelations earlier in the afternoon had him readjusting far too many assumptions about her. Her own struggles helped her with her patients, and her kindness and concern for his father surprised him. She consistently advocated for his dad, even if it meant pissing them both off.

He shook his head, baffled by Amanda Hayden. She didn't appear to be anything like her father, but how could that possibly be? The man practically raised his kids on his own. That greediness and power had to have rubbed off.

Maybe Amanda's coma changed her like Dad's stroke changed him. He had no idea if that was a thing, but if it was, that could explain it. Actually, what he knew of Bill Hayden, that could be the only explanation.

Turning back to the sink, he washed-up before opening the fridge and pulling out the ingredients for meatloaf. He set the oven to the right temperature to give it time to heat. It used to be one of them had to ride in early to make dinner, but with Dad showering before dinner, it gave him extra daylight to get work done.

Mashing up the special low-fat meat was satisfying, and he made a mental list of what to tell his dad. He hadn't been talking with him about the ranch much as he worried it would anger him that he couldn't say anything. But now, he could. The possibilities became endless. Why had he never appreciated his father's input before? It was probably because he and Dad butted heads so much. He was always too busy proving his ideas and suggestions were right. Sometimes he was sure his father argued with him just for the sake of arguing.

He shook his head. Those days might be gone forever. Maybe he could get his dad riled up tonight. He thought of at least three outrageous ideas he could bring up.

After he put the meatloaf in the oven, he realized too late he'd made enough for the three of them, which was a problem since Dad was eating like a cactus wren. Then again, leftovers were just as good.

He heard the water shut off in his father's bathroom. It would still be a good thirty minutes before Isaac had him dressed and ready for dinner. Did Dad feel embarrassed that another person had to help him bathe?

He hadn't thought about it before, but now that Amanda had told him how she had felt, he was beginning to think more about what it was like to be in his father's shoes, instead of how soon he could get better to help *him*. Here he'd thought he was being considerate and helpful, getting all the best help, but now that he reflected on it, he was just being selfish.

He wanted his father to feel needed because he was. But he also needed to sound upbeat, so as not to overwhelm him.

Everything was done just as Isaac stepped into the kitchen. "Hey, that smells good."

He held back a smirk. Isaac always praised his and Brody's cooking because he hoped for some, which he always received. "I've got plenty here. Grab a plate."

"Thanks." Isaac quickly helped himself. "I'll just go sit outside. The sounds in the desert are so much more enjoyable than in the city."

"You mean you like the sound of braying donkeys and mooing cows?"

Isaac opened the slider. "It's a lot better than police sirens and semi-trucks."

He imagined it was. As the slider closed, he pulled out the tray and added his dad's plate to it. Dad was pretty good at feeding himself now, but only if he didn't need a knife.

Quickly, he cut the meatloaf into bite sized pieces and didn't put as much on the plate either. His dad always seemed bummed when he couldn't finish.

Walking in with the tray, he found his father's wheelchair rolled up to the table and his dad staring into space. Amanda called it the "blank" stare. It was better than finding his dad talking to his mom. "I made the tomato meatloaf, though I bet you could tell from the smells."

He got raised brows for his comment. Not a bad start. He set down the tray. "I know you would prefer a beer, but they won't let me serve you yet, so it's iced tea."

Dad picked up the fork, ignoring him.

Returning to the kitchen, he made himself a plate and brought it in, then sat across from his father. Since he didn't want indigestion, he didn't talk, instead he enjoyed the meal. He watched Dad covertly and when the straw in the iced tea almost knocked the glass over, he grabbed it, to keep it from spilling.

He got a grunt for his efforts, which wasn't bad. For some reason, Dad seemed in a good mood. That was never the case when he was around, at least not since the stroke. In the back of his mind, he felt like Dad blamed him for some reason, but that made no sense. It was his father who told people where to go on the ranch and what to do. Maybe Dad resented him taking over. Now, that was a possibility.

As he finished his meal, Dad grunted, and he looked up to find he had cleaned his plate. "You ate it all? You must have had a lot of physical therapy today to work up that kind of appetite."

His father shrugged unevenly, but it was clear he was proud of himself.

Rising, he picked up the tray and walked it into the kitchen, then came back to remove his own plate. He'd love to crack a beer and relax with his father, but that wouldn't be fair. Returning to the den, he wheeled his father back from the table so he faced the unused bar.

Pulling a chair from the table, he swung it around to straddle it.

Dad watched him, obviously suspicious.

"I think it's time I update you on the ranch."

Instead of showing interest, his dad turned his head as if he didn't want to hear. That didn't bode well.

He continued anyway. "We had eleven successful births this week. So far that makes twenty-three with only one that struggled, but all are doing well. We also got the western fence fixed, but found there was a minor rockslide on the south side of the south pasture. A large bolder knocked over a post. Luckily, it filled the gap it left, so no cows have gotten loose. I'm going to have Layne use the backhoe to get that monstrosity off, and we'll get that repaired."

His father still didn't look at him.

Taking a deep breath, he continued. "We were going to start putting the new metal roofing onto the birthing enclosure, but we still have a lot of pregnant cows over there, so I decided to wait. The last thing we need is to stress out those mothers, especially Lulabelle. She'd probably never forgive me."

That got him a grunt, so at least he knew Dad was listening.

"Last week the Town Council asked for a whole bunch of stuff regarding the dude ranch rezoning." He paused, but there was no sound or movement. "I was able to pull all the information together and get their questions answered in time. Then they had me meet with the planning board this morning."

He wasn't sure, but it looked like Dad had stiffened. Was he waiting to hear the result?

"They seemed pretty satisfied with my answers. It's a good thing you left such detailed reports and notes. I read them all. Otherwise, I wouldn't be able to answer anything they asked." He paused, nervous but determined. "My only concern is if they ask anything else, I'll be lost. I didn't prepare everything. You did. It would really help if you could help me get this passed. The dude ranch idea was yours, and as much as I don't like it, I see no other way for us to survive."

Dad finally looked at him, his brows drawn down and his lips pursed.

"As much as I hate to admit it, I need your advice to run this place. You have more knowledge than I do. You have more experience." He smiled. "Yes, I admit it. I need your help."

He waited, almost breathless. Would Dad argue with him? As far as he was concerned, that would be a good sign.

Dad's upper lip curled up on one side and his nose wrinkled. "Worthess."

The single word was said with such vehemence that it

caught him off guard. "Worthless? You mean the dude ranch idea? I don't think so. I think it could work."

"Worthess." Dad used his good arm to press his fist to his chest. "Me."

His heart stopped beating for what felt like a full minute as his brain wrapped itself around what his father meant. A chill permeated his chest as comprehension settled in the pit of his stomach. "What? No, you have all the knowledge. If we are going to save Rocky Road, we have to do it together. You—"

Dad's fist slammed on the arm of his wheelchair. "No." He used his good arm to turn the wheelchair around to face the opposite direction.

Stunned, he sat there staring at Dad's back. No? As in no he wouldn't help. As in no he couldn't help. This was not his dad. Brody was right. The person before him was someone else, someone he didn't know.

He rested his forehead on the back of the chair, the feeling of failure threatening to overwhelm him. He'd finally accepted that his father wouldn't get well one hundred percent, but he could get a lot better. Amanda believed he could, but only if he wanted to. The man he knew would never quit, no matter what.

Angry, frustrated, and losing hope, he rose from the chair and shoved it back under the table. Then he strode out without another word. In the living room, he knocked on the window to let Isaac know his dad was done eating and headed out the front door.

The darkness was lit by the solar lights along the

pathway to the stable, and without thought, he followed it. At the last moment, he walked around the building to face the land that was Rocky Road Ranch.

He stood in the middle of the ATV road heading toward the rest of the ranch. He could barely discern the outline of the two peaks to the north. The darkness resonated with his mood. He felt as if he'd fallen into an old copper mine and no matter what he did, the ground kept giving way beneath him as he tried to climb out. He needed help, and the one man he'd hoped he could depend on, the one man he'd always depended on, refused.

A wild burro honked in the darkness only to be answered by a screech owl. The sounds struck a chord. Is this how his dad felt? Like he couldn't get out of the darkness? Like he had no help? But he had a lot of help. Unless...

A shiver ran up his spine. Unless Dad didn't want help because it would be easier to be with Mom. For the first time he allowed the thought to take root, and it grew quickly. If the man inside wasn't the father he'd always known, then he might give up. The shock of that realization had his eyes itching. He'd already lost his father. A sharp pain struck his chest so hard that he pressed his fist against it. Now it felt as if that old mine was caving in on top of him.

He forced himself to see the shadows, the walls of the stable, the fence of the corral, the giant arms of the saguaro cacti standing sentinel on the hillside. The ranch ran for miles, and he loved every rocky piece of it. He clenched his hands, refusing to lose it. He refused to lose Dad as well. Amanda said a psychologist could help, so that's what he would do. He wasn't giving up on the ranch or his dad, even if he had to shoulder it all himself. This was his entire life. Without it, he was nothing.

A coyote howled in the distance before the desert returned to its nightly silence.

Amanda left the den with a smile on her face. If Jeremiah needed help coming to terms with his condition, and understanding that he still had much to live for, he now had the best help available. She'd called in a big favor, but it was worth it. Jeremiah had so much potential if he'd just get out of his own head.

Closing her laptop that sat on the island, she slipped it into her satchel and left it there. No one knew her password, so it was safe. Striding out the front door, the heels of her cowboy boots kicked up the desert dust as she made her way to her borrowed truck. After grabbing her cowboy hat from inside the vehicle, she slammed the door. She donned her hat and strode toward the stables, the heat of early morning Arizona reflecting off her white button-down shirt. She didn't mind it in the least. A desert cowgirl through and through, she planned to enjoy that part of herself today.

She was in the best mood. Not only had Tanner agreed to a psychologist for his father, but Jeremiah had started talking more. Granted, it was mostly to complain, but it was progress. That he felt comfortable enough with her to talk made her happy. As far as she knew, he wasn't talking to anyone else. She made sure Dr. Navarro knew that before starting today.

Stepping into the stables, she stopped, listening for any sounds. Sure enough, she could hear Tanner talking to his horse in the last stall. Yesterday, Brody had let it slip they were moving cattle today and how difficult it would be because they were down three men. She moved forward, halting when she reached Fury's stall, Tanner already tightening the cinch strap on his saddle.

When he finished, he rose.

"Hey, need some help today?"

He whipped around at the sound of her voice. "Why?"

She set her hand on her hip and rolled her eyes. "Let's see. Because you're moving cattle and you're shorthanded?"

He frowned, which was exactly what she expected, which just made it harder to keep from smiling at him. "Brody told me."

His shoulders relaxed. "That sounds like Brody. What about Dad?"

"He's in with Dr. Navarro." She motioned with her thumb over her shoulder. "I am definitely not wanted. So I thought I could help you instead."

"Are you offering to ride?" His brows rose, clearly skeptical.

"I am." She grinned. "I may be rusty, but I'm better

than having no one to chase down strays or bring up the rear."

His gaze ran from the top of her hat to the bottom of her jeans where they met her boots. "Fine." He turned back to Fury and walked him out of the stall to loop the reins over the door. "Let me just get Maximus saddled." He gave her a stern look. "We already know you can handle him."

She bit the inside of her lip to keep from laughing outright. The man seemed to only have two modes, not happy, and grumpy.

Luckily, he turned away and she covered her mouth with her hand. She followed him to the stall of the majestic Maximus and hung her arms over the half-door to watch him work. He was not only efficient, but thorough. He wore a maroon-checkered button-down shirt, blue jeans that hugged his butt quite nicely where a red bandana peeked from his back pocket. His brown boots looked well-worn, though his straw hat looked new. Nothing about his clothes matched and yet they fit him perfectly.

She grew up with cowboys all around her. Even her brothers were all cowboys, so she'd married a lawyer. But watching Tanner work was actually a pleasure.

He finished getting Maximus ready and walked the big black Quarter Horse out and down the barn toward Fury. The two horses eyed each other, but behaved. "Are you coming?"

Her cheeks heated at being caught staring. She strode forward. "You bet."

"There'll be no time for lollygagging around. We're getting a late start because Layne found Mrs. Silva on the side of the road with a flat tire. If the work is too much or the heat starts to get to you, just let me know before heading in. I don't want anyone getting heatstroke on my watch. We're in for another triple digit day. The sooner we can get this done, the better."

"Got it." She grasped the horn of the saddle as she set her foot into the stirrup and threw her leg over the horse's back. Maximus was much bigger than her horse Breeze, which she rode in her barrel racing days. She was glad she'd been practicing with Breeze for the exhibition because the first week of practice she'd been sore after not riding for months. The last thing she wanted was to look like a wimp in front of Tanner Dunn.

Tanner mounted up. "The cattle have been grazing on the northwest corner. We head past the birthing enclosure and take a right. We're moving them to the southwest corner today. Waylon will have the gates open. He and Nash will ride drag. Brody and Layne are already out there. I'll be riding point. We're still short three men, so it's not going to be easy."

She gave him a short nod. "Got it, Boss."

He studied her as if he wasn't sure it was such a great idea that she help, but finally he clicked his tongue and set Fury into a relaxed pace.

She followed at first, but the day was so beautiful. Wispy white clouds drifted high in the sky and the temperatures had yet to reach a hundred. Unable to curb her energy, she brought Maximus up to Fury and looked over at Tanner. "Race you to the birthing enclosure." She gave her big horse a nudge and they shot off.

Laughter bubbled up inside and she let it out. But as she heard pounding hooves behind her, she urged Maximus faster. "Come on, boy. I know you're as happy to stretch your legs as I am."

She heard swearing as she and Maximus shot forward. Her hat flew back, the tie holding it behind her. Even her ponytail was coming loose, but she didn't care. This feeling is what life was all about.

"Stop!"

Her focus on the upcoming enclosure, she was startled to find Tanner racing beside her.

"Stop, now!"

The fury in his voice indicated something was seriously wrong, and she quickly slowed Maximus. As they came to a walk, Tanner brought his horse closer.

"What's wrong?" She let her gaze run over Fury. Did he throw a shoe, step in a hole?

Tanner brought Fury around to halt Maximus, which the stallion did not appreciate, but she kept him under control. "It's okay, Max."

"I'll tell you what's wrong! You could have broken your fool neck. Or worse, could have ridden Maximus into a groundhog hole and broken his leg!"

Broken her fool neck? Who spoke like that anymore? "What are you talking about? This is the path you and your men take every day. I doubt very much that there are any hazards along it."

Still, he glared at her as if he was trying, unsuccessfully to calm down. "There is no reason to court trouble." The words were ground out as if pulled from the depths of his six-pack abs. "A ranch is a dangerous place. Anything could happen." As he spoke, the words seemed to come easier. "Safety should be paramount at all times. Accidents happen. A charging bull, a broken cactus, a fall." His mouth closed as if he'd almost revealed too much.

Her brothers rode hell bent for leather on a regular basis, and if she wasn't mistaken Brody had been a trick rider for a while. He must have taken a bunch of falls learning that. It wasn't as if she'd been—wait, fall? His father had fallen from his horse when he had the stroke. Could that be why Tanner was so upset? Was he worried about her? The thought made her heart warm.

"I apologize." Maybe she could help him understand. "Since I finished rehab, I've always tried to make the most of every moment of life. There was a time when it looked like I would never ride a horse again. That I can, fills me with joy. What seems a simple ride out to move the cattle is a chance to treasure the freedom of movement, fresh air, and beauty of the desert."

"It's dangerous." His grumpy attitude was in full force now. "If you want to help, I can't be hindered by your foolishness. Now, will you listen to my orders or do you want to go back to the house?"

No one had spoken to her like that since she was in

college and her father made it clear no men were allowed to stay the night. She'd packed up the next day and moved out. She couldn't exactly do that now with Tanner, but she could go back to the house and let him fend for himself.

Yet even at the thought of turning around, she longed for the task that needed to be done. It had been so long since she'd moved cattle. She kept silent longer, making him wait, pretending to decide which she preferred to do.

"Well, are you coming or going?" The words were said by a man at the end of his patience.

"That's a difficult decision, but since it's such a perfect day, and Max is such a great horse," she patted the stallion on his shoulder, "I think I'll come with you." She smiled as if she didn't know he was in a full fury. Hmmm, there was definitely something to the names of the Dunn's horses after all.

Without another word, he turned Fury around and started forward at a relaxed pace. She followed sedately, unable to help grinning. The man needed to loosen up. He was strung tighter than an exercise band around a barrel.

Her humor evaporated at the thought. She'd figured out early that he loved his dad and would do anything to get him back to his very best, but she'd neglected to think about what a burden that had placed on the oldest Dunn son.

Surely, he'd been trained to run the ranch. Her own brothers, as crazy as they were, ran the ranch with her father barely helping. Bill Hayden gave direction on occasion, usually asking if something had been done yet. That was always a serious hint, but he barely rode out anymore. Yet Jeremiah had been riding out and from the sounds of it, he rode daily. Now, Tanner had to take on those duties, and being short-handed didn't help. No wonder he was stressed.

She'd just have to prove to him that she could be of help.

As they rode up, the men came in to get instructions. Brody grinned at her. "What, Dad isn't enough of a challenge for you? You want to take on my brother?"

She rolled her eyes. "No. Your father has another specialist with him and didn't want me around. Can you imagine that?"

He shook his head. "I don't know. I'll have to try."

"Alright. Let's see if we can get this done sometime before midnight." At Tanner's announcement, she pulled her lips in like she'd been caught doing something wrong.

Brody choked on a laugh, coughing instead. "What's the plan?"

Tanner gave everyone direction, sending her to the flank position to catch strays as she expected. At first it wasn't hard prodding the cattle forward, but eventually, one decided it preferred the grass on the north side better then moving on and took a sharp turn.

She was on it, herding the wandering bovine back in line before another broke ranks. She wasn't sure if it was the Dunn cattle that had stubborn minds of their own or it was just that it had been a long time since she'd herded cattle. Either way, it was over an hour before she had a breather, able to look up and pay attention to something other than a cow's ass.

Tanner was up front on the east side guiding the herd, Fury listening to his commands as if they thought alike. She smiled. No doubt they did. He yelled across to Brody who changed his direction, keeping the herd closer together. Maybe the cows were growing tired, but they all fell in line for a while. Tanner stopped, pulling the bandana from his back pocket and wiping the sweat from his brow as the herd continued along.

He glanced back at her.

Quickly, she gave him a thumbs up.

He gave a curt nod before yelling at one of his hands to watch a bull.

She had to give credit where it was due. Tanner Dunn knew his way around cows and horses. He looked damn good doing it, too. The luster of cowboys had worn off a long time ago for her, though her friends in college were always angling for a chance to come to her ranch when she went home for visits. They were practically googly-eyed over her brothers, who didn't think twice about showing off, not to mention sleeping with her friends. She always had to make new friends because she couldn't stand the old ones putting her brothers on pedestals.

She couldn't see Tanner showing off for anyone. He just did what needed to be done...safely, of course. Had that started after his dad's stroke or was he always like that? She'd have to ask Brody. She wasn't exactly on Tanner's good side right now. Then again, she *was* helping.

Maximus suddenly stopped in his tracks. Immediately, alarms went off and she scanned the ground. Her heart thudded hard in her chest. A diamondback rattlesnake had slithered out from under a mesquite tree, no doubt to find out who was making such a ruckus during his afternoon nap.

She kept perfectly still, watching the snake as it looked at Maximus. In her peripheral vision, she noticed another cow stroll away from the herd, but she had more important matters to attend to. This would be a great time to have a gun on her. Unfortunately, even if she did, she wasn't the best shot.

The snake's head swiveled looking around to see if anyone else was about, but seeing no one, it settled back to staring at Maximus. She could feel the horse's muscles tense as he instinctively knew the danger he was in. She wanted to back the horse up, but she wasn't sure if Maximus would listen.

"Don't move." Tanner's voice was soft, but it still startled her.

She moved her gaze only from the snake to where Tanner sat on Fury about ten yards away. He had his rifle trained on the snake.

"When I shoot, Max will rear. Hold tight."

She understood and gripped the reins without moving them, hoping Tanner was a better shot than she was.

The next ten seconds as she watched the rattler seemed like hours as sweat trickled down her back and sides. Then as if the snake had realized it had more company, it lifted its head higher to look at Tanner.

The shot went off, and she gripped Maximus with her thighs and leaned forward as his front hooves left the ground. She was a good horsewoman, but it had been years since she'd had to deal with a rearing horse, and she grabbed the pommel to keep her seat, having no idea if the snake was still a threat. As Maximus gained his feet, she turned him away in case the snake still moved.

"You're good." Tanner hopped off his horse.

She brought Maximus back around and watched Tanner stride toward the snake. It made her nervous that he could get bit, but as she coaxed Maximus a little closer, she could see the snake was just twitching, its muscles moving after its death. Tanner kicked it under the tree then walked toward her. "You, okay?"

She opened her mouth, but no sound came out. Swallowing hard, she tried again. "Yeah." She patted Maximus on his shoulder. "This is one good horse."

He looked at her, but didn't say anything. Instead, he turned and walked back to Fury. Once mounted, he pointed to the east. "Two cows went that way."

Of course. Back to work. As she turned Maximus in the direction he indicated, she felt her heart palpitate and her hands started to shake. "Shit." She let Maximus choose his own pace and in no time, they caught up with the cows.

She looked toward the herd, which had gone quite a ways, no doubt almost to the southern area. "Hold up, Maximus." She pulled on the reins. When the horse stopped, she wiped the sweat off her palms onto her jeans and took a few deep breaths, trying to get herself back on track. When she was ready, she clicked her tongue and started herding the two wanderers.

Of course, upon getting close to the bovine, they split and went in different directions, making her task that much harder. Eventually, she got them headed the right way, but by now the rest of the herd was already resituated. Not about to give up, she coaxed the two forward.

Hoofbeats pounding the ground ahead of her had her looking up to find Tanner returning. He probably was wondering what took her so long.

But as he rode up, he didn't say anything, just stayed on the other side of the two cows and helped her get them where they needed to go. Everyone else had returned to the house by the time they got the last two into the southern pasture. As Tanner closed the gate, she admitted, if only to herself that she was exhausted. She rode up to where he stood and slipped from her horse.

Her knees buckled under her and she made a grab for the saddle.

Tanner leapt forward, catching her about the waist. "Hey."

She shook her head even as she found her footing with his help. "I'm okay. Just got a little shaken. I didn't treasure the idea of having to tell Jeremiah his horse got bit by a snake."

His arm wrapped around her, and she clasped him about his waist with one arm as he walked her to the fence.

He was a solid post of muscle compared to her weak knees.

As he stepped back, she used the fence to lean on. "Just after-scare jitters. I'll be fine." She grinned. "Nothing a good dinner, some ice cream, and a hot bath won't fix."

He stood there scowling at her. "I don't like seeing diamondbacks where the cows have been grazing. The last thing I need is to have to treat a cow for a snakebite."

She cocked her head. "You're kidding, right? We live in the desert. They live in the desert. It happens."

He took his bandana from out of his pocket and wiped the sweat from his brow before setting his hat back on. "Yeah, but I still don't like it. I especially don't like it when they become a threat to my horses or workers."

She probably knew the answer, but she had to ask. "How did you know I was held up by a snake?"

He gestured toward the north. "I saw a cow leave the herd and when you weren't on its tail, I looked for you. I saw you just sitting there, and I knew something was wrong. It wasn't until I rode closer that I figured out from your posture that you had a snake problem."

"Well, I'm glad you're a better shot than I am." She grasped the fence rail tighter as she remembered the moment. "I had no idea if I could get Maximus to back up. Honestly, at that point, I was just hoping the snake would decide to slither back into the shade."

He rested his hand on the rail next to her as he shook his head. "That wasn't happening. That snake had you in his sights. He could have bit you as easily as Maximus."

Despite the heat of the day as the sun climbed to its zenith, she still shivered. "I haven't been that nervous since I went to my prom in a wheelchair." She attempted a laugh, but it sounded pathetic.

"I'm glad you held your seat. A fall from Maximus can be just as dangerous as a snake bite." His voice lowered, sending bubbles bouncing around in her stomach.

"Yeah, I thought about that, too."

He cupped her face with his hand. "I'm glad you weren't hurt."

She licked her lips at the intensity in his green gaze. "I'm glad, too." Her heart started to beat faster as he lowered his head and brushed his lips against hers, sending a tingling down to her toes. Her breathing hitched, and she opened her mouth to take in air.

Whether she meant it as an invitation or not, he took it, his mouth pressing to hers as his tongue slipped between her lips.

Just as before, his kiss sent fireworks shooting to all parts of her body, exciting her from the inside out. His leather and sage scent filled her nostrils even as she leaned into him. She tangled her tongue with his, wanting more of him.

As if he felt the same, he turned to face her, his hand moving to the fence rail on the other side of her as he pushed her against it, his body harder than the wood behind her. Every womanly area of her body woke up as if from a deep sleep and celebrated the feeling of being wanted.

She looped her hands around his neck, as liquid fire filled her limbs. She wanted him. Pressing her hips to his, she felt the hard ridge in his jeans that told her he felt the same way. Immediately, her core ached, and need climbed up her back.

His mouth left hers, but before she could groan her displeasure, he was kissing her neck in the one spot that dropped all her inhibitions. Her knees began to weaken all over again, and she held on, not willing to miss—

The ring of his phone filled the air, waking her up as if her alarm had gone off. She reacted similarly, too groggy to understand exactly what it meant. Still, she managed to move her hands from around his neck and let them rest against his hips.

Tanner sighed, lifting his head, but he didn't back away. Instead, he reached into his back pocket and answered as he looked at her. "Yeah."

She could hear a voice, but not what was said.

"Alright. I'm coming in now."

She smirked at his wording. Didn't she wish.

He put the phone away still looking at her as if he was trying to figure her out, his hand returning to the fence on the other side of her. He was always so careful. Sometimes the man just needed to enjoy life for what it was.

"We have to head in now."

She'd figured that out already, so his comment made her want to laugh, but she managed to keep it in. "Too bad. I liked where this was going."

At her words, his eyes darkened.

Her heart skipped a beat as every nerve-ending came alive.

He pulled her hard against him and kissed her with such intensity, that all she could do was hold on. When she was breathless, he broke the kiss, and stepped back.

She grabbed hold of the fence to steady herself.

"Thank you."

For what? The kiss? She stared, not comprehending. Who thanked someone for a kiss that was mutually shared?

He took another step back as if being so close was too tempting. "We couldn't have made the switch in pastures so quickly without your help. You did good."

For some unknown reason, his praise filled her with pride. Now that she knew what he was thanking her for, she could find her balance. "It was fun. I don't get to work on a horse as much as I used to. Except for barrel racing exhibitions, I don't get much riding in."

He visibly stiffened. "Barrel racing? You could get hurt."

"Only if I didn't know what I was doing. But I do. I've been doing it for twenty years, the last five just for exhibitions, not true competitions. Trust me, I'm good." She pushed away from the fence, quite sure there would be no more kissing...for now. She had to admit she hoped there would be another opportunity. Who would have guessed?

She walked by him, tempted to smack his tight butt, but refrained. "You should come see the races during Pioneer Days. I open them as the announcer explains the rules and the goal."

He shook his head, grumbling something under his breath as he mounted Fury.

She squelched another chuckle as she swung her leg over Maximus, happy the horse hadn't been hurt.

As Tanner turned Fury toward the trail, he brought his horse next to hers. "No racing."

"Spoil sport." She grinned, pretty sure she heard him snort before he flicked the reins and set a relaxed pace back to the house.

CHAPTER 6

TANNER RODE in from the western fence line, his mind on Amanda as usual. It had been a week and a half since their kiss and he couldn't stop thinking about it, or rather her. Even his dreams were filled with pushing her against the fence before undressing her and entering her right there where they stood. That's when his practical mind interrupted and told him it was hotter and dirtier than the picked over bones of a dead burro in August and there was no way that could happen. Waking up frustrated, he had to take care of things for himself, which just pissed him off.

Amanda was a Hayden, and as much as his mind knew that, his body didn't give a shit. Her sunny disposition was beginning to wear him down. Even now, he couldn't wait to get Dad his lunch, just so he could see her. He was pathetic.

Riding up to the stables, he jumped down from Fury's back and gave him some much needed water. Tying the reins, he quickly headed for the house. He wasn't sure if it was her doing, or he was making more out of the touches she gave him, or reading into how her rounded ass brushed his own as she moved past him in the kitchen. But like a dog in heat, he was anxious to find out. That she had called him and asked him to come a little early because she had a surprise, was like lighting kindling in a drought for him.

He stopped before opening the door. What the hell was wrong with him? It wasn't like she was going to ask him to meet her in his office for a quick tumble.

Even as he recognized his own weakness, he reached for the door. Stepping inside the air-conditioned entryway cooled his head as he dropped his hat on the front table and slowed his walk, breathing in the light scent of vanilla that let him know she was in his house.

"Oh, I think I heard the front door. Are you ready?" Her voice was louder than usual.

He heard a grunt which could only be his dad. Suddenly, the idea that the surprise had to do with his father registered and a different kind of excitement filled him. Striding quickly into the kitchen, he continued into the den to find his father sitting in his usual spot before lunch. "I came as quickly as I could."

Amanda in her scrubs, rose from the chair she'd been sitting in at the table. "You mean as quickly as you safely could."

Surprised by how on target she was, he frowned. "Yeah, that."

She laughed. "Don't worry. We know. And now your father would like to show you something, but you have to promise not to move from where you're standing, no matter what."

His whole body rebelled at the command, but he forced himself to nod.

"Good." She moved to the two parallel bars that he had ordered before Dad came home.

As far as he knew, they were just gathering dust. Immediately, his guard went up.

"Okay, Jeremiah. Show Tanner you plan to ride Maximus again one day."

Dad gave him a lopsided grin then put both his hands on the wheels of the wheelchair and rolled himself to the bars.

He stood in shock. Dad always used just his good arm. When had he learned to use the other to wheel himself?

Dad set himself up between the bars and rose on unsteady legs, but Amanda was there, not touching him, but ready if he fell.

It was all Tanner could do to not rush over and help, but Amanda hadn't only been helping Dad over the last week. She'd been educating him as well, and explaining what he needed to do and not do. Or rather, she and the psychologist. So he forced himself to remain where he was, even as his father gripped the bars.

When Dad took his first step, he felt such a surge of pride that his eyes itched. Then there was another step before Dad backed up and sat again with Amanda's help.

"What the hell! I'm blown away." He clapped. "You've

obviously been doing a lot of work while I've been out with the cattle."

"I have." His father grinned, not a sly smile, but a real one. "Betta watch yer step boy."

He swallowed hard at the phrase Dad had uttered almost on a daily basis before the stroke. "I always do with you." His throat closed as his father wheeled away from the parallel bars and rolled up to the table. "Weres my foo? I'm ungry."

He swallowed past the lump in his throat. "Gotta make it." He spun on his heel before his father saw the tears in his eyes.

As he fixed the chicken salad sandwich from the leftover chicken the night before, he tried to wrap his mind around what his dad had accomplished. The psychologist was really helping. Did that mean he might have his father back soon? He wanted to go right back in the den and ask Dad for advice on a snag they encountered inspecting the beams for the new roof on the birthing enclosure, but he forced himself to finish making lunch.

Amanda had just told him two days ago that the worse thing he could do is try to rush his father's recovery. Still, the possibilities of how his dad could help him flooded his brain, and he almost put ketchup on the sandwich. He lifted the bottle up just in time, leaving a red drop on the counter. Hell, he needed to slow down. Wiping up the mess, he switched out the bottle for the low-fat mayonnaise and finished the sandwich, cutting it in two like Dad liked.

He added a glass of lemonade to the tray and started

for the den, wondering why it was so quiet in there. As he crossed the threshold, he halted, his father's chin was on his chest. He'd fallen asleep. Startled, he looked to Amanda, who motioned for him to go back in the kitchen with her hand.

His heart filled with love for his dad at the realization of how much effort walking had been for him.

Amanda didn't lower her voice. "Now, Jeremiah, I think we should decide on your next goal. Dr. Navarro said you always have to have a goal if you want to make progress, right?"

He heard a weak grunt.

She chuckled, the sound filling him with contentment. "Maybe we need to work on getting rid of your grunting. You're definitely not a pig with how little you eat. More like a cardinal bird."

"Teet, teet." His father's voice sounded louder. He must be waking up.

"Tanner, I think your father is getting hungry. He's tweeting like a bird. Either that or a broken alarm clock. I'm not really sure."

As he strode back into the room, Dad stuck his tongue out at Amanda.

"Dad!" He set the tray down on the table. "You always told us never to do that."

His father just shrugged. Then with both hands, lifted half the sandwich and took a bite.

Amanda left the room to have her own lunch. He never saw anything in the fridge that she brought from home, so he had no idea what she ate. Maybe one of those protein shakes or something. He grimaced at the thought as he took her seat.

"Wuts wrong?"

At his dad's question, he shrugged, purposefully mimicking his father. "Just thinking about what to make for dinner. Brody's going to a wildlife exhibition to talk to the game rangers, so it's just me tonight."

"Steak."

He grinned, beyond pleased that his father was taking an interest in life on the ranch again. "Steak. It would have to be sirloins. The ribeyes are thicker and won't defrost in time." Not to mention they were considered off his dad's new diet.

Dad grunted.

Barely biting back a smile, he raised an eyebrow. "I'm guessing you'll want mashed potatoes and broccoli?"

Dad finished chewing and took a sip of lemonade, still using the straw, but his hands were steadier. "Peas."

There were peas in the freezer. "I can do that. Anything else?" It was the first time Dad had requested a specific meal.

"Bed." Dad shook his head. "B-r-ed."

"What kind? I've got sourdough or rye. Or I can make biscuits."

"Bikets."

This time he did smile. "Sounds good to me." He rose to pull out the steaks. "Is that it?"

Dad shook his head. "Mandy."

His heart stuttered at Amanda's nickname. "Do you mean Amanda?"

His father nodded before taking a big bite of his sandwich.

"You want Amanda to stay for dinner?"

His father nodded again.

"Well, I can ask, but I make no promises. She usually has things to do in the evenings." Actually, it seemed like every evening she had some event to attend whether it was barrel racing practice, a baseball game, dinner with friends, a balloon ride, and who knew what else.

Suddenly irritated, he headed out of the room. It seemed that everyone had a life beyond the ranch. His step slowed as he entered the kitchen. That may be true, but he loved Rocky Road. The thought of getting dressed and going out held no appeal to him at all.

"How's he doing?" Amanda sat at the kitchen island typing notes on her laptop.

He found himself smiling again. "He's doing great." He moved to the fridge and opened the freezer. "He wants steak for dinner. First time he's made a meal request."

She stopped typing. "Oh, that *is* good."

He took the steaks out and set them on a plate to defrost. "Yeah. He had another request."

She gave him a sly smile. "Let me guess. He doesn't want you making it."

"What?" At the light in her blue eyes, he realized she was teasing. "No. As a matter of fact, he thinks I'm an exceptional cook. His other request was that you join us for dinner."

"Oh." Her smile faltered.

For some stupid reason, his gut tightened as disappointment filled him. "Don't worry. I told him you were always busy in the evenings."

"No, it's not that at all. I have no plans for tonight." She squinched up the right side of her face, which was never a good sign. "It's more of a boundary between work and personal life. To have dinner with a patient mixes that up a bit."

For some reason her explanation relieved him. "Then call it dinner with me. I'm not your patient. Besides, we need to celebrate my dad standing up and walking for the first time. It wouldn't have happened without you. You figured him out and used your expertise to bring him this far. I worked with him every day of my life and I know how hard that is. This is as much your accomplishment as his."

She blushed. "I appreciate your acknowledgement."

He swallowed hard, not used to admitting when he'd misjudged. "You were right. I asked for the best and I got the best. You know your stuff. In all honesty, I owe you a dinner. So I'm asking you to allow me that privilege. If I bring him to dinner too, then you really haven't crossed the line."

Her eyes rounded then a slow smile lifted her lips. "That works for me. What time?"

"I usually feed Dad early when it's just him and me, but what would be good for you?"

"I'm all for eating early. Would five-thirty work? That would give me a half hour to change and relax."

"Five-thirty it is." His mood brightened considerably at having a guest for dinner. And why wouldn't it? It had been months since he'd cooked for anyone besides family. "Just so you know, I don't do any of that fancy cooking. Just simple ranch stuff with a few spices my mom liked."

She held up an empty wrapper of a protein bar. "Anything is better than this."

He frowned as he opened a cabinet and took out the biscuit flour his mother had always used and set it on the counter. "Is that what you eat for lunch every day?"

She nodded. "It's quick and filling, but not exactly interesting."

He held his hand up. "I promise your dinner will be better than that thing."

She chuckled even as she tried to look behind him at the box he'd taken out. "I'm going to hold you to that promise."

Smiling, he headed back into the den to give Dad the good news, but he found his father sound asleep in his chair, the sandwich completely gone.

For the first time in a long time, he felt happiness. He didn't want to examine the feeling too much. Instead, he wheeled his father back from the table and lifted the tray. Could things really be turning around for them all?"

As he returned to the kitchen, Amanda closed her laptop and put it away. "Is he asleep?"

"Yes. But look." He held up the empty plate.

"Oh, that's good. He did work hard today. I think I've found the right amount of work for him. Dr. Navarro is very good. Without her, I don't think he would have made any effort at all, but it's like he has a new lease on life."

She slid off the stool. "I have to go to my car, but I'll be right back. He should be asleep at least an hour."

He watched her walk out of the house. Had he and his father really just asked a Hayden to stay for dinner? As he loaded the dishwasher, he couldn't believe it. Then again, Dad didn't know Amanda was a Hayden.

But he did. And for some reason, it didn't seem to matter. He was as excited about cooking her dinner as he'd been on his first date at the ripe age of fourteen. He shook his head at himself. He was either an idiot or very lucky. He wasn't quite sure which. All he knew was he'd be sitting at the table with a very pretty woman who could ride a horse with the best of them and still kiss like there was no reason to stop.

He closed the dishwasher and wiped his hands on the kitchen towel, suddenly stopping in midmotion. "Hell." He was going to kiss her again tonight and the only thing that could stop that from taking place was her.

After hanging the towel on the hook, he headed for the door, grabbing his hat as he went. He opened it to find Amanda just three feet away, and he halted.

She stopped too. "Oh, sorry. Just needed to get a

change of clothes for tonight." Giving him a wink, she brushed past him and into the house.

He closed the door and walked toward the stable whistling.

Amanda wheeled a sleeping Jeremiah into his bedroom where Isaac waited for him. She kept her voice low. "I'm afraid we may have worked him a little hard today. That and the dinner he almost finished tonight did him in."

Isaac put down the book he was reading. "Not to worry." He kept his voice low as well. "I'll get him washed up and in bed before he realizes it."

She smiled. "Thanks." As she strode back into the kitchen, her boot heels made noise on the travertine and she quickly switched to walking on tiptoe. Tanner was wiping the counter down after having cleaned up. She had to admit it was a treat to have such an amazing dinner made by a man and then not have to help with clean up. It was odd how different the Dunn brothers operated after losing their mom compared to how her own brothers operated after her parents divorced. Was it because her family had more money or because they had her as an older sister? It wasn't as if she'd done much cooking, so she had to chalk it up to her father hiring a cook.

She hopped up on a stool at the island, knowing she should be leaving soon, but not really in any hurry to go home. "That was really good. Thank you again."

Tanner hung the dishtowel on the hook and set his palms on the counter. "It was Dad's idea, but I'm glad you stayed. It was a great way to celebrate. Maybe you can bribe him with staying for dinner next time he balks at doing something."

She liked that idea more than she should. Still, she rolled her eyes. "That won't work. You told me he's only motivated by completing something he starts."

"True." He turned pensive. "But that was before the stroke. There seems to be a lot that has changed in him, including his personality."

Now that was intriguing. "In what way?"

"This may sound stupid, but he's nicer than he was before. He's more like the dad he was before Mom passed. I thought people with strokes often turn...well...meaner."

She shook her head. "There's no one way. Actually, I don't think the stroke is what changed your father. I believe he was the same, though I can't be sure, but with Dr. Navarro's help, he's finding himself again. Did he ever go to grief counseling after your mom died?"

His eyes rounded. "Dad? Hell no. He's a 'pull yourself up by the bootstraps and get on with life' kind of person."

She nodded, having met way too many people in the town of Four Peaks who were exactly like that. "Well, whatever it is, I'm thrilled he's doing so well."

Tanner studied her for a moment. "You really do care about him."

She felt her cheeks heat. "Yeah. I know. Crazy, right?

It's my one flaw when it comes to my job. My supervisor is always telling me I get too emotionally invested."

"I don't see it as a flaw. I actually think it's what makes you so successful. Don't let your supervisor take away your superpower. He'll be sorry."

She chuckled to hide the glow of pleasure his compliment gave her. "She. My boss is LaReina and she's pretty good. She knows when to motivate me and when to back off."

"Back off?"

"Yes. She can be pushy sometimes, especially when I want time off. I give my job one hundred and ten percent, but when I need a break, I need it. In fact, after I get your father to a good point, I'll have three months off."

"What would you do with three months off? I think I would lose my mind."

She didn't doubt it. "That's because your work is your home and hence your life. Mine isn't." She scanned the homey kitchen area. "Though, sometimes I miss this. It's not the same at my father's and when I get my own place, it still won't be home." Now why did she bring up her father and her wish for a real home?

The quiet was interrupted by a yell. "Kent make me!"

Isaac's voice followed. "Jeremiah, stop. I *can* make you, but I won't. You tell me what you want to do."

Tanner moved out from behind the island. "Would you like to take a walk?"

Though she probably shouldn't, it took less than a second to slip off the stool. "That would be nice."

Instead of heading out the front door as usual, he moved into the family room and opened the sliding glass door that led to the backyard and pool area. He held his arm out for her to precede him. "The temperature is half a degree cooler out here."

She laughed as she stepped outside. It was still very hot outside compared to the air-conditioned house, but the whole area was already in shade as the sun began to set. She walked along the edge of the pool to a covered area with two lounge chairs. She sat back in one. "When was the last time you sat in one of these?"

He lowered himself onto the one next to her, sitting on the side of it as if it would bite. "I don't think I have, but Brody has."

She swung her leg over the side and sat up to face him. "Did your father ever come out here and enjoy them?"

"Once. Brody cooked barbeque out here and Dad sat on one to eat dinner." As if he felt he needed to defend himself, he quickly added to the explanation. "Mom was the one that insisted on the pool and covered space. I do use the pool, when the water isn't too warm."

She scrunched her face. "So in the winter?"

He smiled. "Yeah."

She rose because he was obviously not comfortable, and they continued toward the back of the walled in area where there was an opening. His heels on the concrete assured her that he followed. She stepped past the open wooden door at the back and found herself looking at two of the Four Peaks. They were bathed in a golden glow with just a bit of orange flame starting. Even her dad's ranch didn't have such a beautiful view. "Wow, this is spectacular."

He stepped up next to her. "Yeah. It's part of why Dad thought we could turn the place into a dude ranch. He figured the pictures Brody could put up on a website would entice people to stay here."

She turned toward him, surprised. "Your dad wants to make Rocky Road a dude ranch?" The local cattle ranchers laughed at people who did that. She was shocked.

He didn't look at her, just kept his gaze on the mountains. "Yeah. It's the only way we'll be able to save the ranch." He finally turned his head and met her gaze. "The big cattle ranchers are pricing us out. We don't have enough land to expand. We are bordered by the conservation land your father put in place and one other piece, whose owners refuse to sell even though they are doing nothing with it."

She swallowed the lump in her throat at the mention of her father. Was that what started the feud?

Tanner turned back to the mountains. "I searched the internet for other ideas, but I couldn't come up with anything else, so we either become a dude ranch or sell and leave. I don't like either prospect, but Dad wants to try the dude ranch."

Her mind spun with the news. Then she remembered the paperwork he'd been sifting through one afternoon. "That's what all those plans were?"

He started to walk toward the mountain, his footsteps

crunching on the dry desert earth. "Yes. In order to become a dude ranch, we had to request a change in the zoning. I have no idea if it will go through. I don't want this place to change, but it looks like it's change or give it up."

Her heart sank at the tone in his voice. He really didn't want the change, and she felt for him. It never occurred to her that the Rocky Road was too small to survive. She walked beside him as the possibilities of what a dude ranch could do filled her head. "Wow, your father is brilliant."

He stopped suddenly and looked at her. "Because he wants to change this place to survive? That's not brilliant. That's desperate."

"Yes, well, maybe. But just think of all you could offer and how much you can educate the average person who never had a chance to grow up in a small town like ours." Ideas began popping in her head like popcorn on movie night. "Besides horseback riding, you could offer hiking, archery, barrel racing, roping, traps, target practice, hayrides, in addition to educational activities like gun safety, lectures on the flora and fauna, even snakes." She grinned, becoming energized at all the options. "At night there could be campfires, singing, making s'mores, plus I'm sure one of the girls in town would be willing to teach some line dancing. Heck, you could even have Town Nights."

He halted, his brows raised as he stared at her in surprise. "Town Nights. You know we'll be a laughing stock in town for having a dude ranch, right?"

She waved off his comment. "Maybe at first. But on Town Nights you could have a local band and invite people for a special price. You could even do haunted hayrides. We don't have any of those. Oh, and just think of how your ranch alone could put Four Peaks on the tourism map. Right now, all we have is Pioneer Days, but your place could be open all year!"

He groaned, shaking his head. "And when do we do our work? We do have cattle to raise and bring to market."

"You really haven't looked into this have you?"

At the shake of his head, she held her hands out to the sides. "That's the beauty of a dude ranch, the paying guests help with the work."

"Whoa, they don't know a thing about cattle ranching."

She laughed, too excited by the project his family was about to embark on to contain her enthusiasm. "They don't have to. How would you like twenty extra people loading hay into the barn? Need the horse stalls mucked out? Teenagers would be great at it. Have a loose heifer? Bring along three dads who want to feel like they're real cowboys. Seriously, Tanner, this is a fantastic opportunity not only for the Rocky Road Ranch, but Four Peaks as well." She smiled at him, unable to stop. It was phenomenal.

"I didn't realize." He stared at her in a daze, obviously seeing the positives of his father's idea for the first time.

She took his hand in hers and pulled him forward as they walked around the outside of the house. "Do you see the possibilities?"

"I guess." His voice was quiet. "It's a whole new staff

and schedule and paperwork. Not to mention the budgets and books."

She stepped in front of him, halting their progress, his hand still in hers. "If you're looking for backers, I'd love to invest some money."

His left eyebrow lifted. "You would? Don't you think your father would have something to say about that. Besides, the Town Council still needs to approve the rezoning, and that's not a done deal. It's not like they've voted in our favor in the past."

She stared at him. What else had the Dunn's requested? Had it been when her dad was on the Town Council? It seemed she would have to ask her father how the feud had started after all. She'd lived her life in ignorance, trusting him, but after getting to know three of the four Dunn men, she had to wonder. "Well, if they vote in favor, I will be the first to invest. I also know some pretty wealthy people in Phoenix who would see the advantage of this place. You say you are too small to compete, but being small is a great place to use for a dude ranch."

Smiling, she tried to will him to see the vision she saw. *Come on, Tanner. Look beyond what you know to what could be.* She waited, hoping to see something in the rosy light of the setting sun, darkness descending quickly. Letting go of his hand, she put her hands on either side of his face. "Imagine nine-and-ten-year-old boys and girls on top of horses, excited to ride out to see the calves that have been born and help feed those with no mama. See parents sitting beside their kids as they chow down on barbeque ribs while an old timer from town tells them what life used to be like on a ranch before ATVs."

He stared at her as if he wanted to believe, when suddenly his eyes widened.

"See it?"

His lips lifted into a slow smile. "I do. I see it. We can focus on the past so it's not forgotten."

"Yes! And next time they have steak for dinner, they'll know where it came from."

Before she realized what he was about, his arms came around her and his lips pressed against hers. She opened her mouth, her excitement at the ranch's future quickly morphing into another excitement altogether.

There was something about Tanner Dunn that called to her. She wasn't sure if it was his command of the ranch or the command he had over her sex drive, but kissing him felt so right. No. More than right. Heavenly.

He backed her up as if he couldn't get close enough. When her back came in contact with the outside wall of the house, a flare of desire shot straight to her core. Claude tried doing something similar with her once, but it was pure play acting. Tanner's need for her was as real as her need for him.

She grabbed his butt and pulled him closer, letting him know she wanted him.

His mouth left hers and he looked at her as if trying to understand why they were so attracted to each other, but she didn't want to understand.

She yanked his checkered shirt out from the back of his

jeans and ran her hands up his back. "Kiss me." Though she'd meant the words to come out as a demand, they were barely above a whisper.

The man must have excellent hearing because his mouth descended onto hers with a fury, his tongue taking over.

Her heart raced as heat filled her and need raced to the juncture of her thighs. She slipped her hands inside his jeans, loving the hard yet smooth feel of his taut butt cheeks.

He broke their kiss and grabbed her hands, pulling them out and lifting them over her head, capturing her wrists with one hand.

She looked at him with wide eyes, not a little surprised, but his nostrils flared just before his mouth found the side of her neck that caused her to melt.

She closed her eyes and let her head fall back against the warm adobe wall as his mouth lowered to her collar bone. Somehow, he managed with one hand to unbutton her shirt and his tongue traced her breast along her bra line. She arched upward, wishing she hadn't worn a bra to dinner. When her bra loosened, she opened her eyes, but all she could see was his dark hair as his lips moved her bra aside, and he captured her nipple in his mouth.

A groan left her and she rose on her toes, loving the feel of his mouth gently sucking her. She wanted to tell him not to stop, but the words were drowned out by the pleasure tightening her stomach. When his mouth moved to her other breast, she lowered back down to her heels, not unaware that his fingers were working the button of her jeans. She sucked in her breath, giving him room and within seconds his hand moved along her abdomen, past her shaved mons, and down to her moist folds.

He seemed to hesitate at her readiness, but she didn't want him to. Swallowing hard, she forced a word from her lips. "More."

As if that was all he waited for, his fingers moved farther and found her clit.

Her sheath tightened in anticipation. Yes! The thought was there, but the word wouldn't come as her breaths came faster.

Then his teeth found her nipple and rolled it, sending sparks straight to her core. That's when his finger moved expertly between her legs, gently rubbing her clit to send shockwaves of pleasure deep inside her. When his finger slipped from her favorite spot, it moved inside her sheath, and she bucked toward him, gasping for air as need riddled her body like buckshot.

He slipped his finger out and added a second, even as his thumb circled her clit. It was all she wanted, and she arched into him, her panting turning to moans. His mouth left her breast and caught her own. His tongue invaded her like his fingers as he pressed her hard against the wall, sending her spiraling out of control.

Her orgasm burst through her like a rampaging bull, propelling her into ecstasy, sending pleasure to every part of her as she floated in excited bliss. Eventually, the thrills subsided, finally allowing her to take slightly deeper breaths.

When she was able to focus on her surroundings, she felt Tanner's mouth leaving a kiss on her outer ear, his hand cupping her between her legs, while he still held her arms above her. "Wow." Her voice was raspy and her breaths were still short, but she felt him smile against her cheek.

Then his mouth moved toward her ear again. "I want you."

His gruff words buckled her knees, but his hand between her legs held her up. She'd never felt so wanted by anyone in her entire life, which sent her heart back into race mode. She licked her lips, swallowing hard, determined to answer.

She turned her head toward his ear. "Then take me."

His body turned to stone against her, stopping her heart for a moment.

CHAPTER 7

TANNER FROZE, fighting the craving that urged him on. This was Amanda, kind, caring, intelligent. But even that reminder didn't help. He felt like an oversexed bull that couldn't control his own need. Her words didn't help, giving more than permission, demanding he fill her. It was more than he could resist.

Reaching between them, he unbuttoned and unzipped his jeans, something in the back of his mind telling him to stop, but unable to listen. He couldn't even seem to let go of her hands as he pushed her jeans from her hips, not bothering to take them off her.

Pulling his cock out, he held it to her moist folds, still trying to retain some semblance of a man and not a beast. But her scent filled his nostrils and his hips pushed forward, sliding into her. He breathed in as he was surrounded by wet warmth. Entering her took the sharp edge off and allowed him to hesitate.

She wriggled against him and it took him a moment to realize she was attempting to toe-off one boot.

As much as he didn't want to, he slipped out, pulling back far enough so she could slip off her boot. He held down her jeans as she pulled her leg out.

Before he could move his hips, that leg wrapped around him.

He didn't need any more urging. Holding his cock, he pushed between her folds once more, but this time he slid all the way in. It was pure heaven. Then he pressed his hips harder against her, pressing her to the wall as he filled her until he was buried deep.

And still it wasn't enough. He took her mouth with his, thrusting his tongue inside as he slid almost all the way out and back in.

She moaned, her foot pressing against his ass.

His balls tightened as need raced up his spine. Quickly, he moved his hand to her breast, pressed and squeezed her hard nipple gently as he thrust back in.

Tiny whimpers filled his mouth, urging him on. He thrust in again, harder this time and her hips met him halfway, sending him to the edge. He refused to come without her reaching her peak as well and he squeezed her nipple a bit harder.

She broke their kiss on a hiss, and her foot urged him back in.

Squeezing her nipple again, he thrust, and then again, and again, losing track of where he ended and she began, pulling them along together up a mountain of pleasure until her sheath tightened around him.

"Yessss!" Her cry as her body sucked at him, ignited his orgasm, and he pulsed into her, unable to stop.

It was pure bliss, taking him from physical being to something else, something filled with pleasure and joy. He wanted to stay forever, but his body expended itself.

Even as he slowly came to his senses, her rapid breaths brushing by his ear, he wanted nothing more than to hold her, keep her close, not let her go. As he released her wrists, her arms wrapped around his shoulders. He gathered her tight against him and nuzzled her neck, the scent of vanilla mixing with their sex.

He wasn't sure how long he held her, but she didn't move, except for her chest as her breathing slowed. Finally, she lifted her head from his shoulder. "I don't want to stop."

Her words made his cock move inside her, and he pulled his head back to look at her. Darkness had fallen, but a slight purple still tinged the sky behind him and reflected on her face. Her lips were swollen from his kisses and her cheeks were flushed. "We don't have to."

She smiled. "Good. But maybe we could go to your room?"

At the realization he'd just had sex with her up against the wall of his home, he had to make it right. He wasn't sure what had happened. He looked past her at the window not three feet from where they stood, and grinned. "Actually, this is my room. Just the wrong side of the wall."

She laughed at that, which sent vibrations through both of them. She gasped. "Well, maybe we could continue on the other side of the wall?"

At first, he tried to reconcile the sweet Amanda who cared so much for others with the sexy vixen in his arms and couldn't until he remembered her saying she wanted to live life to the fullest. He grinned at her, relieved that she may not have seen his rutting as an insult. "If you like, I'd be happy to use the other side of the wall."

Again she laughed. "Oh, I don't care where in your room, just as long as we are in there and not out here where Brody might come upon us when he arrives home. If I'm not mistaken, his truck lights would put us in a spotlight here."

He looked over his shoulder to see that she was right. She was right about a lot of things, and they really should move, but he didn't want to leave her warmth. He moved his hands under her bare ass. "Then hike that other leg up on my hip and we can go inside."

Her eyes rounded and then her smile widened. "I like the way you think." In the next instant, her other leg wrapped around his waist.

Unfortunately, his jeans had fallen to the tops of his thighs. With one hand at a time, he pulled them up far enough to be able to walk and quickly moved to the front door. Hoping Isaac was busy with his father, he got them inside and into his room without being seen.

"Wow, you're good. Now which wall is it?" She looked behind her as if she could figure it out.

But he wasn't taking her on a wall again. He moved to his king size bed and sat near the pillows, not far from the plain walnut headboard which was about as tall as he was sitting there.

She gave him a sly smile. "You know, eventually, we'll have to separate."

He frowned, not liking that idea at all.

Her brows raised. "I didn't mean now. Lie back. It's my turn."

Intrigued, he did as she said, his feet still planted firmly on the floor.

She leaned to her left, bringing one knee to the side of him before leaning to the right to do the same with the one that still had her jeans and boot on. "Now, you just relax and let me ride."

At her announcement, his cock inside her moved again and her eyes widened.

"Oh, you like to be ridden. Who would have thought?" She pressed both her hands on his chest to move into the perfect position.

He laid his hands on her hips as she adjusted, her movements causing him to start to harden inside her. Surprised by that, but not about to question his sex drive at the moment, he lifted his chin. "Let's see what you can do from there."

"Now that sounds like a challenge."

He grinned, thoroughly enjoying this sexy side of her.

"Do you have voice command lights?"

He shook his head. "No. Why would I? I'm perfectly capable of turning on my own lights."

She chuckled. "Of course, what was I thinking? But in this position, you aren't capable, are you?"

"I can if you want me to." He didn't mind moving with her sitting on him.

She shook her head. "No, no. I can reach the lamp." Leaning over, she proved she could, and a mellow glow filled the room. "That's better. I want to see you."

He was far more interested in seeing her, but since she had accepted his command of her body so willingly, he would do the same for her.

"First things, first. We have on too many clothes."

He silently agreed, even as she shucked off her unbuttoned shirt and threw it on the floor. Then she pulled off her bra and his abdomen tightened. Her breasts were each a perfect handful, the areolas colored a dark rose. He lifted his hand to touch her, and she grabbed it. "Nope, not yet."

Not pleased by that, he began to seriously rethink letting her be in charge.

"Now your shirt."

Guessing she expected him to take it off, he lifted his torso off the bed high enough to get his arms out, but that meant that he also lifted her up as well. When he had it off, he left it on the bed beneath him and dropped back.

"I do believe you have an eight-pack under there. That was impressive." Her hands found his abdomen and she traced his stomach muscles with her fingertips, which had his cock taking notice inside her. She felt it because her lips quirked up, but she didn't say anything.

Her hands moved past his abs and over his chest before resting on his shoulders. "I knew you had strength but I would have never guessed this much. I like it." She smiled slyly as her hands moved to his nipples and she tweaked them.

His stomach muscles reacted as well as his cock.

"Oh, I like that." She leaned over him and taking his head in her hands kissed him.

He tried to let her lead, but it just wasn't in his nature and he soon invaded her mouth as he cupped her neck.

She pulled away a bit breathless. "Okay, I get it. You're not the submissive type at all. I guess we can both be in control." She sat up on him, which sent him deeper into her, something he was more than happy with.

Taking each of his hands in hers, she placed them on her breasts. "They're all yours."

He didn't need any other coaxing to gently squeeze her perfect orbs before brushing her nipples with his fingers.

She pulled her arms back, arching into him, reaching her hands behind her to play with his balls.

Hell. Sharp shards of need shot through him. Quickly, he began to roll her hard peaks between his fingers.

Her eyes closed, and she started to move against him. Not up and down, but forward and back, and he understood her need.

With his feet planted on the floor, it was easy to lift his hips high.

Her eyes opened wide and she grabbed hold of his arms. Her hips continued the motion as her head fell back, her breathing coming in quicker pants.

He could feel her getting close as he held her there, keeping his attention on her even as his own need to release rose.

Her hands squeezed his arms hard just as she tightened around him and a high-pitched moan filled the room.

She was beautiful as she burst apart on top of him, her body rocking uncontrollably as she milked out every possible moment, but as her sheath began to relax, he brought his hips down and rolled her over.

The motion nestled him between her legs and he began to thrust, his own orgasm on his back, coming closer, and closer.

Then her hands gripped his ass and squeezed. That was the final touch that pushed his release past his control. As it swept through him like a haboob, he held her tight, knowing she was his anchor back to reality. Once he spent himself inside her, he finally pulled out and rolled to his side, trying to catch his breath.

She followed him and laid her head on his shoulder, but didn't say anything, her own breathing still not quite normal.

His hand found her hip, and he held her against him, the position so natural, he didn't think twice about it. There was something about Amanda that was like coming home. That made no sense, since he spent the better part of his life avoiding her. The last thing he'd expected was to have sex with her. But she was an attractive woman, despite being a Hayden. That had to be why he'd acted like a rutting bull. Who wouldn't around such a vibrant, beautiful, adventurous woman? Coming inside her sweet—

"Ah, hell." Every muscle in his body tensed.

Her head came off his shoulder and her brows raised. "What? Did you forget something?"

He looked at her, unable to reconcile his actions. "I forgot protection. I *always* use protection."

Her face relaxed. "Not to worry. I'm on the pill and haven't had sex with anyone since my divorce, so you're good. Believe me, after discovering my snake of a husband was cheating with his manicurist, I got tested immediately."

He rolled away and sat up. "No, I'm not good. I'm always careful." He turned his head to look back at her, somewhat dumbfounded. "Always."

She sat up and moved to sit next to him, her bare legs, with her jeans and one boot dangling over the side of his bed. "Do you mean to say that somehow I distracted you and you forgot to be cautious?"

The excitement in her eyes had him standing, pulling up his jeans and walking to his dresser before turning to face her. "You don't understand. I have to be careful, always, or people get hurt."

Her brow lowered. "I'm not hurt. It's okay." She bent over and pulled off her boot, letting her jeans fall to the floor.

He shook his head. "It's not okay. You don't understand."

She scooted back on the bed and sat with her legs crossed. "Then tell me. Help me understand."

He stared at her, sitting absolutely naked, ready to listen. He didn't remember the last time someone actually *wanted* to listen to him. She was too hard to resist on many levels. He bent down and picked up her shirt and handed it to her. "Fine. But put this on. I can't talk and look at you naked."

She grinned, appearing quite proud of herself, but she did as he asked. "Okay, I'm covered. Now tell me why you must always be careful."

The problem was, he wasn't sure if he knew how.

She could see Tanner struggling. His jaw worked as if he were talking with it closed, but no words came out. He shifted his weight from one leg to the other and back again.

Her instinct told her this was important, and the fact he was willing to share it with her was not lost upon her. Could it be that he didn't really know why? "When did you first realize you needed to be careful?"

His movements stopped as if she'd given him a place to begin. "I was nine." He leaned back against his dresser, his gaze far away. "Devlin was eight and Jackson was seven. We were in the barn. A new hay delivery had come in and they were building forts with the bales. I, of course, was attempting to get the barn ready for more hay."

The self-loathing in his smirk made her heart stop.

"I always had to be just like Dad. So I told them I was going up to move the bales in the loft, so he could bring more in after lunch. I thought I knew exactly how they should be organized." He shook his head. "Dad and I will never agree on that."

She bit down on a grin. It sounded as if Jeremiah and Tanner had started their contentious relationship very early on.

"So I went into the loft and started rearranging bales." His gaze moved to her. "You have to understand, these bales were half my weight at the time, so it was more that I dragged and heaved to get them where I wanted them. There was really no lifting involved."

She nodded, understanding completely. Even as a teenager, moving bales had left her with sore muscles.

His jaw clenched and he looked away again. "I wasn't paying attention. Next thing I know, Devlin and Jackson are in the loft with me, moving bales around to create a fort. I told them they needed to get down. Dad didn't allow anyone in the loft until they were nine. Jackson stuck out his tongue and said Dad wasn't there and asked if I was going to be a tattletale. Devlin just shrugged and said he'd be nine in a couple of months so it didn't matter."

Tanner stopped talking.

She found herself clutching her hands together, her heart racing at what was to come. She'd completely forgotten there had been a Devlin Dunn, and her gut told her she was about to find out why.

Finally, he spoke again, but his voice had dropped in tone and volume. "One wall of their fort was near the edge of the hayloft. I was too busy being mad at them to pay attention. When I finally did, it was just in time to see Devlin throw a haybale on top of another, lose his footing, and fall into them sending them and him over the edge." Tanner's hands closed into fists. "Even as he yelled, I thought for sure he'd land on the hay and not the cement floor. I rushed to the edge, expecting him to be laughing, but he wasn't. He didn't move."

She wrapped her arms around herself, not wanting to hear the inevitable end to the story, but knowing she had to. Her eyes began to water and her vision blurred.

"I climbed down the ladder and raced to him, but even at that age, I knew in my gut. His head was at a wrong angle. But I still hoped. I didn't know he'd broken his neck." Tanner looked up as if seeing the scene. "Jackson started yelling. Asking if he was okay. Demanding that Devlin be okay. I stood between Devlin on the floor and Jackson in the loft and told him to run and get Dad. As Jackson came down the ladder, I hunched over Devlin to keep Jackson from seeing, yelling at him to just get Dad." Tanner's shoulders slumped. "They said he died the second he hit the concrete."

Tanner took a deep breath then finally looked at her. "It was my fault. I should have insisted they stay below where it was safe. Dad made that rule for a reason. I still don't know why I let their name calling get to me. If I'd been man enough, Devlin would still be alive."

She swallowed hard, knowing that crying for Devlin wasn't what Tanner needed. "Did your parents blame you?"

His brows lowered. "No. They said it was an accident. But they weren't there. Jackson told them everything and apologized, promising never to go in the loft again if only Devlin would get better. They took Devlin away in an ambulance, so even I had hoped, but a few days after the funeral, Dad told me the truth. Mom said I did everything right, but she was wrong." He banged his fist against the dresser. "There were many things I could have done differently and if I had, I'd have Devlin here right now."

Her heart ached for little Devlin, but even more for little and old Tanner. "I understand that feeling. That feeling like somehow in the past, if we could have just seen the future even though right now, we are clueless about it. If I had known that going to Cattail Cove and staying into dusk might cause me to get bit by a mosquito which would lead to me going into a coma, I would have chosen to leave earlier or not go at all. But I had no crystal ball. Still, it seems like just one small decision could have avoided it all."

He crossed his arms. "You think that's what I'm doing?" Everything about him said he was affronted from his scowl to his tense abdominals.

She leaned back on her hands and studied him. "Yes, that's what you're doing. You're blaming yourself for something you couldn't foresee. You can bring it back to the beginning of the day and say you should have told your dad that Devlin needed to stay home. Or better yet, you should have had the sugar puffs cereal instead of super wheats, so Devlin couldn't have any, so he would throw a tantrum, and stay home with your mom instead of going out when the hay was delivered."

"Men don't throw tantrums."

"No, but boys do. Any number of events could have prevented what happened, some of them in your control, some not. My guess is your father bears a far larger burden of guilt over that. It must have broken his heart to tell your mother."

Tanner's eyes widened as if that had never occurred to him.

She completely understood. It had taken her years before she thought about how her dad felt about her illness. When she found out he blamed himself, she'd blackmailed him into seeing a psychologist. It had definitely helped with his guilt. Not so much his ego though. "So yes, I believe you are blaming yourself for not being able to see the future." She crossed her arms, not willing to budge on her opinion.

He stared at her a long time, then his shoulders relaxed and he uncrossed his arms. "I never thought of it in that light." He walked back to the bed and sat on the edge. "You make me look at a lot of things differently."

Ignoring the thrill his admission sent to her heart, she

shrugged. "I do that a lot. It's a curse." She shrugged again and gave an exaggerated sigh.

"Wiseass." He turned and pushed her back on the bed. "That must be why I'm looking at you differently now."

Her heartbeat doubled at his admission, finding a similar feeling in her own. "You are?"

He grinned. "Yes, like the fact that you look even better without your shirt on."

An odd stab of disappointment shot through her before she gave him a cheeky grin. "Well, I like looking at you better without your pants on, so there."

His left brow raised. "Don't you think we should look our best?"

She pushed him off her and sat up. "Bet I can undress faster than you."

He jumped from the bed without answering, and she quickly pulled her shirt up over her head only to find him standing there in all his naked glory. And what glory it was.

———

Amanda woke with her head on Tanner's shoulder and her leg thrown across his. Even as she recognized her surroundings, her tension eased. Should she have stayed the night with a Dunn? No. Was she thrilled, happy, and satisfied she did? Absolutely. She grinned. They had made love two more times, talking in between. He'd even gone to the kitchen naked and made her a midnight snack. No man had ever done that for her.

She wasn't sure which she enjoyed more, the conversations or the lovemaking. She'd like to think of it as just sex, but she knew what she was feeling. She was falling in love with Tanner Dunn. It was not a good thing on so many levels. First, he was a Dunn. Second, she was his father's therapist. Third, he was a cowboy, the kind of man she promised herself years ago she would never fall for after seeing how her brothers were with women and after dating a couple cowboys before deciding to go to college.

If Tanner was such a terrible choice, then why did she feel happier than she did on her graduation day, wedding, day, and divorce day all combined? Probably because he was a good man. Okay, so he was a stubborn ass too, and sometimes she felt like banging his head against the wall, especially her first month dealing with him. But those moments had lessened, and he did seem to respect her input more now. He also had more compassion than she usually saw in a man. He even listened to her. No, he didn't always agree with her, but he did listen and think about what she said, even changing his mind on occasion. The fact that he'd listened to her views on his guilt over his brother Devlin showed real character.

His story did reveal a lot about the man. He was a protector. It explained why he felt responsible for his dad's stroke, as if he could have prevented it, and why he'd yelled at her for racing. It must have made him both angry and nervous when she and Maximus found the snake. He wanted everyone to stay safe, and it wasn't surprising after his brother's death, his mother's death, and his father's stroke. As the oldest, he already had that "responsible" gene. She knew what that was like. It was hard to shake.

But Tanner had *responsibility* to the tenth power. She understood him so much more now. He was so opposite of her ex. Claude was all about himself. He could have cared less that she could ride or that she had her own career. She was his arm candy and his ticket to important people who could help him advance. It was odd that she'd married someone so much like her own mother even though she had only been eleven when her mother left her father.

Tanner though not only appreciated her career, but understood it and thought she was quite good at what she did. He was the first man to pay attention to that and it meant a lot more than she realized.

His hand, which rested on her hip, moved, idly stroking her. She kept her breathing as normal as possible, curious what he would do.

"Manda." He whispered the word as if to see if she were awake. "Manda, we need to get up."

She snuggled her face against his chest and held him tighter, her knee rising to brush against his package.

His whole body tensed at her touch. "Amanda, time to wake up." This time his voice was normal except for the slight gruffness underlying his tone.

"Hmm." She lowered her leg but stroked her hand over his hard chest. "Do I have to? I had the best dream."

"You can tell me all about it at breakfast."

She looked up at him. "Oh, I don't think my dream would be very good table conversation."

His sudden intake of breath expanded his chest beneath her hand. "Then we'll save it for another time." He patted her hip. "If you want, you can sleep longer. I have to shower and get to work." He lifted his arm from around her and rolled out from under her head and leg. Throwing the blanket off him, he rose, relaxed in his nakedness.

She rolled over, leveraging herself on her elbows to look her fill. "Hmm, now that's a morning view I can enjoy." She licked her lips purposefully, thrilled to see his half-erection jerk.

He stepped toward the bed and bent over it. His hand slipped behind her head as he kissed her thoroughly. Then he stepped back while she tried to slow her racing heart. "I'll be back." Though his words were innocent enough, his voice had deepened after his kiss.

"Thanks for the warning." She winked at him.

He just shook his head and walked out the door butt naked before closing it.

Throwing the covers off, she jumped from the bed and grabbed up her shirt. Luckily, she had toiletries in the truck since she never knew when she'd go to a friend's after being out and about. That's where her clothes for last night's date came from. They weren't her usual uniform for her day's work, but they were clean. Pulling on her jeans, she looked around for her other boot. Where was—oh. It had to be outside. Even as she remembered how anxious Tanner had been to have her, her whole body warmed. There was something about being wanted for her and no other reason that had her smiling.

Leaving her one boot in the room, she walked out of the room barefoot and padded down the hall before stepping out the front door. The cool morning air was dry but pleasant as the sun had not peaked over the mountains yet. Walking along the front porch, she stepped off at the end and made her way around the back. It didn't take long to find her boot on its side against the adobe wall. She picked it up carefully and shook it to make sure it acquired no tenants in the night. She really didn't want to share her boot with a tarantula, scorpion, or snake. She placed her hand against the wall. It was no longer warm, but it had been downright hot last night.

She should feel guilty about spending the night with Tanner. She must have it bad that she couldn't imagine having walked away. Turning, she started toward the front of the house again. She could look at it as a one-night stand, but she'd be lying, and she didn't lie. The question was, how did Tanner look at it? Was it a one-time thing or the start of something new? She shivered but not from the cold as her bare feet touched the stone that decorated the floor of the porch. She would just have to find out.

She jogged down the steps and strode across the dirt toward her truck. Quickly, she grabbed her toiletries and closed the door as quietly as possible. She returned to the porch and opened the front door, stepping inside. The smell of bacon greeted her and she inhaled, already growing hungry. Walking into the kitchen, she expected Tanner, but Brody was at the stove cooking. Oops. Quickly, she turned around and headed for the hall on silent feet.

"Amanda?"

Brody's voice had her hesitating. Quietly, she set her boot down and peeked around the corner. "Morning, Brody."

He stood there staring at her, the tongs in his hand dripping bacon grease onto the floor.

She pointed at the grease. "You better wipe that up. The last thing we need around here is someone falling and me having to provide more physical therapy." She ducked back down the hall. As she passed the bathroom, the sound of running water greeted her. She halted, the thought of joining Tanner in his shower almost too hard to resist, but she grasped her boot to her chest and forced her feet to move to his room. Hopefully, there would be another time for that. He did say he wanted to hear about her sexy dream another time, so that had to mean there would be another time.

Keeping that thought close, she closed the door once inside his room and scanned the contents. Now, what else could she discover about the man who was so into safety but forgot the condoms when around her.

CHAPTER 8

WITH AMANDA safely in the shower, Tanner returned to his room and set the photo album back on his bookshelf. The woman was a snoop, but in all the best ways. He found her laughing so hard at the picture of him covered in paint at the age of seven that he thought she might faint. He grinned as he exited his room. That she wanted to know more about him made him feel like he could oversee the whole town and then some.

When he entered the kitchen, he found Brody had set out three plates on the counter. Did he know the woman was Amanda? Suddenly, his triumphant mood slipped a bit. How would he explain his hook-up with Amanda when he didn't understand it himself?

Brody turned with a large Navajo pottery bowl that their mother always used filled with scrambled eggs and set it on the island. He placed both hands on the counter and looked at him. "Amanda Hayden?"

Surprised, he frowned. "How did you know?"

"Well, her truck was still here when I came home. I figured maybe it didn't start since I have no idea how the Haydens care for their vehicles. But after I saw her peek her head in here, I knew it was her, but still thought maybe she was just early. So I checked the cameras."

Hell, he'd forgotten about the damn cameras he had Brody install.

Brody grinned. "Nice carry."

His face heated, so he turned away and went to the fridge to grab a bottle of water.

"So?" Brody's voice held expectation.

Twisting the cap off, he threw it in the trash and moved to the side of the island with the plates. "So what?"

"Come on, big brother. You don't have a date in like three years and a hook-up in what, maybe a year, and then you sleep with a Hayden?"

There was no censure in his brother's voice, which helped him think somewhat rationally. "I know. It's weird. But it felt right." He took a swig of water before reaching for the eggs.

"Uh-huh." Brody grabbed the bowl away and set a dinner plate over it. "We have company. You have to wait."

"I don't *have* to do anything." Still, as Brody set the bowl and plate back on the island, he didn't reach for it.

"You like her? I mean, more than just her, um, looks?"

He tensed, expecting Brody to say something crude. Not sure why his brother held back, but was glad he did. "Yeah." He paused, not sure how to explain hating an entire family for over two decades and finding himself suddenly having feelings for Amanda. His gut told him it was far more than how attractive she was. He'd actually slept with more attractive women. No, sexy women. No. Just no. "It's hard to explain. Yes, she's attractive but from the inside out. I don't know. All I know is I'm not sorry we did and I want to keep her around...maybe for a long time." Even as he said the words, a sense of rightness settled over him.

Brody's eyes widened and he crossed his arms as he leaned against the refrigerator across from him. "You know you're playing with fire, right?"

"In more ways than you know."

"Be careful. I don't see how this can work out, but they say love conquers all."

"Hey, I didn't say I was in love." Though he did wonder. What he felt for Amanda was far different than anything he'd felt for a woman before. Then again, he'd only had three relationships and they hadn't lasted longer than a few months. A cowboy's life wasn't for everyone, or so he'd told himself as they'd parted ways.

Brody pushed away from the refrigerator and set his hands down on the island again, leaning forward. "I'm no expert. I have no experience in this at all, but I know one thing. You better figure it out quick. Either make it a one-nighter or go all-in because with a Hayden, you either have to be on one side or the other. You know that."

He nodded. What Brody was trying to say was cut off the relationship before it turned into anything so no harm was done, or make Amanda his in all ways, because the only way there was any future was to stand firm against her family. There was reason for their bad blood, but he was able to lay it at her father's feet and not the whole family's. Though what her brothers would think about that, he didn't know.

Pioneer Days were coming up on the weekend. That might be a good time to let Bill Hayden know that Amanda and he were a couple, preferably in a public place so the man couldn't make a scene. He was a politician after all. He wouldn't want any bad publicity. But Amanda would have to be on board, and he had no idea what she was thinking. He was getting way ahead of himself.

Brody suddenly straightened. "Good morning, Amanda. Hungry for some bacon and eggs?"

Surprised he hadn't heard her cowboy boots, he turned on the stool to see she wore her sneakers.

"I'm famished. I think I could eat a whole pig this morning." Though there were four stools and he sat at the opposite end of the counter from the one she usually used, he was stupidly pleased when she pulled out the one next to him and sat. "Do you take turns cooking breakfast, too?"

He nodded, pleased at how at ease she was joining them. "Brody and I just switch off making all the meals each day. Makes it easy. When Jackson finally comes home, it'll be easier as he can take a day, too."

Brody uncovered the eggs and added a large serving spoon to the bowl. "Don't count on it. The minute Jackson gets home, I'm gone."

Brody's reminder that he only stayed until Jackson

came home had become irritating, so he ignored it. Instead, he took the plate of bacon from Brody and offered it to Amanda.

"Thanks. I love bacon." After taking three slices, she pulled the egg bowl closer and gave herself a good helping.

Her appetite fed his ego. He was quite confident her hunger had to do with all the activity last night.

"Oh, I love the spices you put in here, Brody. What are they?"

His brother helped himself, standing on the other side of the island to eat. "Old family secret."

Amanda leaned closer. "You can tell me later."

He grinned that she felt confident he would tell her.

"I heard that."

At Brody's statement, she laughed. "Guess you Dunns have good hearing."

"Even Dad." Tanner gestured toward the archway where he was quite sure his father was just waking. "So be careful how loud you talk if you don't want him to hear. I don't think his hearing was affected by the stroke."

She shook her head as she swallowed. "I don't think so, either." Then before he knew what she was about, she'd hopped off her stool and walked around the counter. "Excuse me, Brody."

Brody moved toward the stove and Amanda opened a cabinet. She pulled out a mug and poured herself some coffee. Then without asking, she took out the sugar bowl. Taking a spoon from the utensil drawer, she added sugar and stirred her coffee before plopping the spoon in the sink.

As she walked around the island, Tanner looked to his brother, who shrugged.

She set down the cup before getting settled on the stool and taking a sip. "Ah, now that's what I need to really get going."

He couldn't help asking, "How do you know where everything is in our kitchen?"

"Really?" She took another sip of coffee and set the cup down. "I have watched you and Brody make your father's lunch so many times, I could find everything in my sleep."

Part of him wasn't sure what he thought about that, but he admitted, if just to himself, that he liked how comfortable she was here. He could almost see her here all the time. The thought tightened his chest, and he quickly scooped up more eggs and bacon.

"So, Tanner." His brother helped himself to another plate of eggs and bacon. "Are we going to get the hay cut in the east pasture for the horses this week or do you want to wait until after Pioneer Days? There's no rain expected."

He'd almost forgotten he'd talked about that. "Let's wait. I don't want to take on any big projects before the celebration. We may have to run into the Town Council again or deliver more information before this weekend. They said we'd probably know by then."

Brody looked pointedly at Amanda.

She waved her hand. "I know all about the dude ranch.

No need to worry. My lips are sealed. Crossing my fingers for you, though." She scraped her plate then pushed it forward. "That was so good. I haven't had a big breakfast since I went to the Rotary's Pancake Breakfast fundraiser."

He stared at her. "That was months ago."

She shrugged. "I'm too busy to cook and my brothers don't leave me anything from the breakfast our cook makes, so I just grab something quick. At least I can sleep in compared to you cowboys." She wiggled her brows, reminding him exactly why she was up so early.

"Speaking of chores, not that you were, but I need to look at that hitch on the horse trailer." Brody dumped his plate in the sink. "Last time we used it, it didn't feel right. It's got to be the hitch or a sway bar. You'll clean up?"

He nodded as Brody strode into the entryway. "I hear Silas Murray is looking for more haybales for his float. While you're out there, see if we have any left he can use."

"Will do."

As the door closed, he found himself alone with Amanda. He should probably say something.

"I'll clean up." She scooted off the stool before he could stop her. "It's the least I can do after having such a great meal."

"Do you know how?" He rose, fully intending to show her where things went in the dishwasher. His mother had taught them all. Even though they were on their third machine since then, they still did it her way. She said it got the dishes clean every time.

Amanda stopped in front of the sink and rolled her

eyes. "Of course I know how to load a dishwasher. It took me months to figure out the best way. It was my chore when my parents were still married. After the divorce, even though Dad hired a cook, I still had to do it until I balked at the age of fourteen." She shook her head. "Yes, it took me three years to get angry enough that my brothers didn't do anything in the house to finally rebel."

Grabbing his half-empty water bottle from across the counter, he stood back and watched her load. When she finished, she turned and held her hand out to the open machine. "How'd I do?"

He stood frozen in place staring at the dirty dishes. She'd put everything in the right spot. He raised his gaze to hers. "You did it right."

She grinned, clearly happy with herself then shut the door.

Amazement filled him. No one loaded a dishwasher like his mom. It was silly to think it meant something, but to him it did. "Amanda."

She stepped up to him and looped her arms around his neck. "Yes, Tanner? Did you want something?" She rose on tiptoe and pulled his head down. "Like this?"

As her lips met his, he wrapped his arms around her as if she were a figment of his imagination and he needed to hold her to make sure she was real. He deepened the kiss, but held back his desire, showing her what she meant to him without words. When he broke away, she stared at him.

"Wow, I felt that right down to my heart." No smile lifted her lips as her blue gaze locked with his.

"It was meant for your heart." He sensed more than heard her intake of breath.

"The feeling is mutual." Her voice was just a whisper, but the words filled his chest like one of the hot air balloons she liked so much.

As he stared into her eyes, feelings of peace and happiness sent a calm through him, the likes of which he hadn't felt in years. *Love.* He knew it for what it was, but couldn't quite say it. Lowering his head once more, he kissed her again, gently, letting her know what he couldn't say.

This time she broke the kiss, loosening her hold around his neck and trailing her hands over his gray-checked button-down shirt, to rest on his abs. Her gaze had followed her hands. "It's a good thing this place is called Rocky Road after all." She titled her head up to look into his eyes as a smile lifted her lips. "Because I have no doubt, we're in for a rough ride."

Yes, she was right, but he didn't even care. He raised his eyebrow. "From what I saw yesterday, you like a rough ride."

She blushed before giving him a fake punch to his stomach. "Behave yourself, cowboy."

As he dropped his arms from around her, she stepped back. "I need to grab my laptop from the truck before it heats up." She looked toward the archway to the den, where talking could be heard coming from his dad's room. "I think I'll tell Isaac I was out with friends, which is why

I'm not in uniform. My employer would frown on me staying the night."

He shook his head. "That makes no sense. Isaac is here almost every night."

"That's different. He's a CNA and sleeps in your dad's room, though I imagine he could probably sleep in the den soon." She pointed to herself. "I, on the other hand, slept in your bed and that would not be cool. Do you think Brody will say anything?"

He probably would. "I'll tell him to keep it between us. In fact, I'll walk out with you and catch him before he rides out."

She turned and headed for the front door. He grabbed up his hat and opened it for her then watched as she walked toward her truck. She had the nicest ass. Once she unlocked the vehicle, he hurried toward the barn. Brody would tell the world without thinking about it.

As he stepped in, his brother was leading Maximus out of his stall. "Brody, hold up." He strode forward, glad he'd caught him.

His brother stopped. "Today's Wednesday, right. It's Maximus' turn."

"Yes. But I need to talk to you."

Brody stroked their dad's horse. "Hold on, boy. Big brother has a problem."

"I don't have a problem."

Brody raised his brows. "Um, yes you do, and it's a big one." He frowned. "Actually, she's not that big, but—"

"Don't go where you're going. I haven't decked you in a while."

"Like you could." Brody grinned. "I was talking about Lulabelle. Why, who'd you think I was talking about?" His smile turned innocent.

Patience. He needed it in spades and for some reason he found it. "Sure you were. Listen, I need you to keep Amanda's night here to yourself for a while. We need to talk about how to navigate this new development."

Brody stopped smiling. "So you really are serious about her?"

"Yes. And I agree with what you said before breakfast." He paused, not sure how to admit what he was feeling to his little brother. Not that he had to, but he deserved to know. Then he remembered how Brody termed it. "I'm all in."

Brody's low whistle caught Maximus' attention and the horse moved forward. Brody pulled the reins. "Whoa, boy. Not yet. That was for Tanner, not you." After halting the horse, he turned back. "If that's how you feel, I'll keep it close to the vest. But it's not going to stay a secret for long, so you two better figure out what you're going to do."

"As soon as we know, you'll know."

"Appreciate it. Now I have to get out to the birthing enclosure. You better saddle up and meet me out there."

Immediately his brain moved into ranching mode. "Why? We have another tough birth happening?" He opened Fury's stall to bring him out and saddle him.

Brody mounted up and grinned at him. "You could say

that. It's Lulabelle. As I'd tried to tell you, you have a big problem today because if you don't get there for the birth of her calf, she's going to scare away what few hands we have left."

"Hell."

Brody laughed before kicking Maximus into a gallop.

Just what he needed. So much for switching lunch duty with Brody, so he could talk to Amanda. The only female he'd be talking to all day was an ornery, lovesick heifer, who thought she owned him.

Amanda threw all her clothes in the wash and strode into her temporary office anxious to finish up her notes on Jeremiah before taking a swim in her dad's pool. She'd been disappointed she didn't have a chance to talk to Tanner the rest of the day. If his kiss meant what she thought it meant, then her life was about to get a whole lot more exciting, not to mention complicated.

Her brothers had already come in, washed up and headed to town. That was typical for a Wednesday night. With the house to herself, she opened the laptop and keyed in the password. Jeremiah was making amazing progress, though she was starting to worry about the damage to his legs. She added a note to order some tests. She didn't want to push him if there was a serious problem. Luckily, he was still making great progress with his speech and both arms.

Finishing her notes, she turned off the computer and closed it. Now for a swim. Crossing the hall to her bedroom, she opened a drawer when her phone rang. Her heart jumped at the thought it could be Tanner, even though he was smart enough not to call her in case her family was about.

She answered the call, which changed her mood considerably. It was an old high school classmate she'd contacted, saying she found the perfect house for her. In no time, she made arrangements to see it on Sunday.

There was a sense of relief knowing she'd be out from under her father's roof soon. That would make her relationship with Tanner a bit easier. Plus, at twenty-nine, she didn't exactly enjoy being back home. Cholla Valley was a beautiful spread, but her life had taken her beyond it. Her brothers were happy here as far as she knew, so that made it easier for her to continue life beyond its walls.

Could it be a life with Tanner? Even as the thought rose, her heart filled with warmth. She could actually see herself at Rocky Road. She could take one of the days for making meals to help. She could continue Jeremiah's therapy as needed, but still keep her career. Tanner would be proud of her and take an interest in it. Of that, she was sure.

After pulling a bikini from her drawer, she closed it. But she had a three-month sabbatical coming up as soon as she finished her work with Jeremiah. The thought of going to Marrakech, Morocco like she'd planned and then flying across the world to climb two volcanos on Maui and the

Big Island lost a bit of luster. It would be fun if Tanner would come, but how could he with the ranch to run?

She sat on her bed. Maybe she could help with hiring additional hands. Then she and Tanner could travel a bit. Maybe even a honeymoon. She grinned at the thought of a week on a beach with Tanner all to herself.

The front door closing jolted her out of her daydream. If it was one of her brothers coming back already, it had to be he forgot something.

She rose to see. It could be her father coming home.

"Mandy!"

At her father's yell, she ran forward. That was not a good sign. Her dad always controlled his emotions, and he sounded seriously upset. She found him in the living room looking out the sliding glass doors to the pool deck. "Dad, what is it?"

He spun around. "Why'd you stay overnight at the Dunn ranch?"

Shocked that he could know where she was, she admonished herself. He had to be guessing. "Why do you ask that?"

He strode toward her. "I thought you were working in Cave Creek all this time, but now I know exactly where you've been. You need to stop. Right now."

"What?" Fear that he had somehow hacked her computer raced up her spine, but she quickly dismissed it. Her father was not particularly savvy with computers. That was her youngest brother. "Why do you think I've been working at the Dunn ranch?"

"I don't think. I know. Rory Lester saw you leaving Black Spur Road. Said he was surprised because it was the fifth time in the last month that he saw my truck out that way."

Four Peaks was far too small. "I can't tell you where I work. You know that. Do you know what kind of trouble I could get into? There are laws around my client's privacy. You of all people should know about laws."

As if he didn't even hear her, he pointed at her. "You are to stop working there right now. I know you're there because it's the only place out that way."

Damn, he had her there. She crossed her arms over her chest and narrowed her eyes. "I will not. I have a contract and I will fulfill it."

His face turned red. "Those are Dunns. They only care about themselves. Whatever service you are providing them is of no importance."

"I provide therapy, Dad." Why is it that none of her male relatives gave a shit about her career?

"I don't care if you provide laundry service. No daughter of mine is working for the Dunns."

She dropped her arms. He wasn't the only one in the family who could be stubborn. "Well, I can't break my contract, so you'll just have to live with it."

His eyes fairly bulged. "Live with it! I will buy out your damn contract if I have to." He stepped even closer, again pointing his finger. "You are not allowed to return to that ranch ever."

Allowed? She was a divorced woman pushing thirty.

Not even her father could tell her what she could do or where she could work. She lifted her chin and stepped closer to him. "I'm not eight years old. I'm a grown woman who can make her own decisions. My decision is to fulfill my contract."

His arm swept out, knocking the vase of fresh plumeria from the end table next to the couch. "Then you are no longer my daughter." He spun away and strode out the front door.

She took a deep breath. Her father had never come close to hitting her, but at that moment, she'd thought he would. Did he really mean she was no longer his daughter? She shook her head. He couldn't. They were close. Closer than her brothers. She was the oldest, his first born, his only daughter.

At the sound of his sedan starting, she moved to the front window to see him hit the gas hard, sending a cloud of dust over the green grass on the front lawn.

A dark foreboding settled in the pit of her stomach. He knew. And if her father knew, it meant he would do something about it. She just didn't know what. Would he go to her company?

No, he didn't even know the name of her company, but he could hire someone to figure it out. It wouldn't be hard. Beneath her anger at his behavior was a deep hurt. Surely his feud with the Dunns wouldn't take precedent over her, his own daughter.

She walked back to her room, unsure what to do. She should probably start packing because he was obviously not going to be reasonable about her position. Picking up her bathing suit, she moved to put it back in the drawer then started for the laundry room. At least she had a place she could look at on Sunday.

But was the damage done? Would her father get her fired? At least he didn't know about the plans for a dude ranch at Rocky Road. Even at the thought of Tanner, her stomach clenched. She'd made this mess. She'd insisted on treating Jeremiah all because a sabbatical awaited her. She just hoped she didn't lose her job before it started.

The next morning, Amanda walked into the kitchen to find it empty, which was odd since the cook was usually there. Glancing at the clock, her confusion deepened. Her brothers should be chowing down right now. Moving to the window, she checked to see which vehicles were parked outside to find the only one there was her sedan. Dread filled her. What had her father done?

Moving to the fridge, she opened it to grab her usual yogurt and halted at the note taped to her breakfast.

Only loyal children are welcome here. It was signed *WH*, not *Dad*, not *Bill*, not even *William Hayden*. Just *WH*.

Closing the fridge without her breakfast, she grabbed some graham crackers from the cabinet and strode to her room. Sitting on her bed, she took out a graham cracker and forced herself to chew. If she didn't get something in her stomach, she'd end up puking, and she didn't have time for that.

She couldn't believe her father would tell her to get out. He'd always been there for her, even when she couldn't feed herself or walk. Yes, he had others do that for her, but he always stayed with her. He loved her. Or so she thought.

Her eyes stung with tears. His hate for the Dunns was more important to him than his love for her? He'd answered that question with one simple note—either be loyal to him or get out. Did he want blind loyalty? If so, he didn't know her at all.

She rose even as she grabbed another cracker. What really burned her was that the Dunns were good people. She knew at least three of the four. None of them were selfish. Maybe Jeremiah had been in the past, but he wasn't now, and maybe he'd changed. Obviously, her father hadn't. And because he hated those good people, he didn't want *her* in his family unless she jeopardized her job and did as *he* wanted?

Anger began to replace the hurt in her heart, and she strode toward the closet, grabbing her suitcase. She threw it on the bed and opened it. Since her father was giving her a choice, she'd make it, and screw him!

It took her no time to pack up her clothes since most of her belongings, furniture, and such, were stored in the garage. Hopefully after Pioneer Days this weekend, she could check out the place her former classmate found for her and have a moving company get her things.

After rolling her suitcase into the hall, she left it there and walked into the guest room, where she found the empty box she'd left in the closet. She gathered her printer, desk knickknacks, supplies, and pictures. One picture was of her when she graduated high school in her wheelchair. She always kept that as a memory of how far she'd come. The other picture was of her dad and her when she graduated from college.

Tears threatened, and she quickly set the picture back down. But then she took it and put it in the box. With her laptop in her satchel, she threw it over her shoulder and grabbed the box before rolling her suitcase to the front door. Setting the box down on the entry table, she pulled out the picture of her college graduation and set it on the kitchen counter. Ripping a piece of paper from the note pad next to the fridge, she grabbed the pen clipped to it and wrote one word on the paper—Bye.

Feeling tears itching the back of her eyes, she dropped the pen and forced herself to go to the door. She'd left Cholla Valley Ranch many times in her life, including to the rehab center, college, and when she got married, but none of those times felt as final as this one. She halted as she reached for the door. Was she overreacting?

The answer came swift. No. It wasn't about whether she was siding with the Dunns. It was about her father not respecting her work or her integrity.

Grabbing the doorknob, she jerked the door open and strode out with her belongings in tow. At least she could look on the bright side. There was now no impediment to her relationship with Tanner. Though the thought did lighten her mood, she hated the fact that she couldn't have both.

She clicked her car open and threw her belongings in the back, then got in and started the car. It was going to be a long bumpy ride to Rocky Road Ranch, but at least she still had her job. As she drove away from the place she grew up, the place where she learned to despise the Dunns, her heart started to lift. Maybe she'd been living too long under her father's judgment and it was time to spread the wings of her mind. As she drew closer to Rocky Road, her mood improved. Already, she couldn't wait to share everything with Tanner.

Maybe between the two of them, they could figure out how to keep her father from causing problems with her job.

CHAPTER 9

"WHAT THE HELL?" Tanner stared at the text on his phone in disbelief, even as rage began to build in his chest.

"What is it?" Brody took a swig of orange juice. "Don't tell me it's the Town Council wanting something dropped off in ten minutes. Idiots."

Tanner looked up from his phone. "Worse." He tried to bring the words together but fury was quickly taking over.

"Hey, watch the pancakes. You're going to burn them."

Quickly, he turned his attention back to his cooking and flipped the flapjacks. "You better take over." He walked away from the stovetop, grabbing his open water bottle and hat as he strode outside.

He didn't even know why he was outside. He wanted to yell at the top of his lungs. He'd been duped. Just when it seemed things were finally going his way, she yanked the rug out from under him, or rather the ranch.

The front door closing behind him had him turning.

Belatedly, he realized he'd been watching for Amanda to arrive.

"Tanner, what gives? I've never seen you like this."

"She screwed me." He lifted his hat and wiped the fast-appearing sweat from his anger off his forehead with his sleeve.

Brody gave him a sly smile. "Well, yeah. I know that much."

He clenched his fists. "No, not that way. She told her father about the dude ranch." He held up his phone. "Bill Hayden lodged a complaint against the rezoning."

"What? He can't do that. He's not on the council."

"It turns out anyone can lodge a complaint, and since, and I quote, 'Mr. Hayden is such a respected member of the community, they need to take his concerns seriously'." He spat.

"Flippin A." Brody rubbed the back of his neck, his demeanor completely changed. "You think Amanda told him?"

He stared at his brother like he'd lost his senses. "No. I think a magic fairy came by and heard us talking about it and then flew straight to Bill Hayden to whisper it in his ear. Of course she told him."

Brody held up both hands. "Okay, okay. I get it. But why? I thought she liked you. I know she likes Dad." His brother crossed his arms over his chest like he'd just made a strong point.

Was Brody really so naïve? "You better get a better sixth sense if you want to be a ranger. Don't you see? She was biding her time until she had good information for her father."

Brody's eyes rounded, but instead of nodding, he cocked his head. "I don't know. She seemed pretty sincere."

His disgust at himself for not seeing it couldn't be any worse than what his father could heap on him. He was in charge. He knew who she was. And he let his twenty-year guard down. His fury at himself tightened his throat, making it hard to speak. "This is going to kill Dad."

Though his voice was raspy, Brody heard him clearly. "Shit."

"Exactly." He stood there staring at his youngest brother, so pissed he couldn't even move. She'd actually slept with him. Pretended she liked him. No wonder he hadn't said the L-word. His gut had held him back. Somewhere in his messed-up mind, he'd known...expected this.

"Standing out here isn't going to change anything. Did the Town Council say what we needed to do next?"

At Brody's question, he blinked. "What?"

Brody turned his hands up and to the side. "Did they tell us what we should do about the complaint, or are we supposed to just sit on our hands and await our fate?"

"I don't know." He looked at his phone again. "It says they're going to send an expert out here to investigate the potential environmental impact."

Brody's brows drew together. "Didn't Dad already have someone do something like that?"

Did he? There had been so many papers. He hadn't

focused on any he didn't need last time he'd emailed them. And when they'd had him come in, the questions were more about the numbers of people and building plans, which he'd studied ahead of time. "I'm not sure. If it was in the paperwork, they'd have it already, so why would they have to send someone out?"

"I think I'll ask Dad. He would know and since he can talk now, and thanks to Amanda, he can answer." Brody gave a short nod before turning on his heel and heading back inside.

Tanner turned back toward the driveway to find the dust cloud he'd been expecting traveling his way. Brody's parting words bothered him on many levels. First, it sounded as if his brother still wouldn't accept the obvious, that Amanda had betrayed them. Second, his dad was sure to ask why they needed to know about the environmental impact. He hoped his brother kept the reason to himself. The last thing they needed right now was for his father to have a heart attack on top of his stroke.

As he watched the dust cloud, he was surprised to see the sedan Amanda had first driven to the ranch. What happened to her father's truck? As she pulled into the yard, he felt her choice of vehicle was fitting as a way to end her job at Rocky Road Ranch. No doubt she'd come to tell him she was done working there. That fit perfectly with what he had in mind.

But instead of her stepping out in a tight red suit and high heels, she bounded out in her scrubs and sneakers. "Hey, cowboy." She smiled before bending over to grab her ever-present satchel. When she straightened, she strode forward as if she expected to kiss him.

He crossed his arms over his chest. "Why'd you do it?"

She halted a few paces away. "Do what? Oh, you mean drive my car over your crazy rocky road? It was my only choice. We definitely need to talk."

"So talk."

She lost her smile and studied him. "I thought *I* had a bad night, but something tells me yours was worse. What's up?"

"I think you know."

She frowned. "No, I don't think I do, unless you heard from my dad."

"You could say that. He's challenged the rezoning."

"What? How could he know about that?"

He stared at her, watching her facial expression as she went from frowning to her eyes rounding. Her hand came to her chest. "You think I told him?"

He dropped his arms. "You can forget the act. I know you told him and that your whole purpose for being here was to find out anything you could that would allow your father to wipe out our operation here. My only question is, does he want the land for himself or is he going with that natural preserve bullshit?"

She wagged her finger at him. "Oh, no. Don't you try to pin this on me. I never said anything to my father about your dude ranch. He probably found out the same way he found out about me working here. Rory Lester saw me exiting Black Spur road. I'm sure someone from the Town

Council told my father. Probably even asked for his opinion."

"Sure they did."

"You don't believe me." Her eyes widened once again. "You actually think I've been busting my butt trying to get your father to the best possible state he can be in, so I could get information for my father? You think I would have you hire the best people there were, even pull in a few favors, so your dad would see if he can improve?" Suddenly, her whole body stiffened. "You think I slept with you just to find out your plans, so I could give them to my father?"

He didn't say anything, careful not to show the holes of doubt she was ripping into his conclusion.

"You do! You son of a bitch! How dare you!" Her gaze was fierce as she scowled at him. "I expected better from you, Tanner. No wonder you can't keep a woman for more than a couple months." She waved her hand at him. "You're pathetic. Don't even know a good thing when you have it. What was I thinking to fall for you?" She readjusted her satchel on her shoulder and started toward the front door. "I'm going to work."

He didn't have time to digest what she said. All he knew was she needed to leave. He stepped in front of her. "No, you're not. You already got what you wanted from us. You can get the hell off my ranch."

She shook her head, her breathing coming fast now. "Oh, no. You are not keeping me from my job. I have had it with men dismissing my career. I'm going to finish helping Jeremiah even if it kills you. Besides, last I heard, this is *his* ranch and he will want me to stay." She gave him a triumphant smile. "So take that, *cowboy*."

The last word was said with such derision that he had to keep himself from stepping backward. What the hell was wrong with being a cowboy?

Amanda brushed by him and pulled open the door to find Brody about to exit. "Oh, hi Amanda. Dad said he has something to show you."

"Thanks." She headed in even as his brother strode out.

"We're in luck. Dad says they already did an environmental impact plan. Guess Hayden is barking up the wrong tree." Brody smiled as if that settled everything.

"Not necessarily. Hayden could convince the council that the risk is too great. I better grab the paperwork and stick it under their nose to remind them a professional has already assessed the issue. And you better get back in the house and watch the other Hayden."

Brody shook his head. "Why? We still have the cameras and it's not like we have any other secrets."

His brother was right. Amanda already knew they were on the verge of losing the ranch, and without the rezoning would have to sell. So Bill Hayden knew it as well, though no one else did, at least not yet. Sure, those in town knew about his dad's stroke. Hell, they even knew Brody had been anxious to do anything but ranching since he graduated high school.

"Besides big brother, you aren't going anywhere for a while. You should be getting a text any minute, and I have to get to the south gate. One of the bulls rammed it and broke a hinge. I'm heading out there right now to help Waylon. At the moment, he's the only thing keeping the herd from escaping." Brody strode toward the stable. "See you out there."

"You go, but I have to head this off at the pass with the Town Council." His phone vibrated and he opened the text. "Hell!" Quickly, he texted back. *On my way.* Following his brother's path, he glanced once more at the house before entering the stable. Why did everything go to shit at the same time? Why couldn't there be shit once a day instead of an avalanche. He was going to be buried in it soon.

Striding toward Fury, he heard the hooves of Chaos as Brody headed out for the south gate. Saddling his horse, he mounted and headed toward the birthing pen. His stomach was so tight he felt like vomiting. How could he have believed Amanda? What was it about her actions that had him falling for her?

Maybe it was how kind and caring she was toward his father. Of course, that would help her get information. But then again, Dad had just started to speak a couple days ago. Maybe that was just how she was in her job. She had seen the plans the day he was frantic to respond to the Town Council's email. But he was the one who told her the whole idea just two days ago. She'd been a lot more excited by it than he was. Because she couldn't wait to tell her father?

He shook his head even as he slowed Fury near the

birthing enclosure. It hadn't been that kind of excitement. She not only thought it a great idea, but seemed to want to be a part of it. Would Hayden close them down so his daughter could run a dude ranch?

Dismounting, he tied Fury's reins to the fence. Amanda's voice floated in his head. *Well, if they vote in favor, I will be the first to invest.* Her enthusiasm seemed real. Then again, so had Dad's and Bill Hayden's friendship. Could she have been so excited she didn't realize her father would sabotage them? She said she had no idea what the feud was about.

If he was wrong, he may have completely blown a good thing. A very good thing.

"Tanner, over here."

At Layne's call, he focused on the issue at hand. Striding to the end of the tarped area, he could already see the problem, or rather part of the problem. The tarp was down along with a metal post. "What happened?"

The man who was at least six years older than him raised his brows. "What do you think happened? Your girlfriend pulled a fast one on us."

How'd his ranch hand know about Amanda and him and what she did? News didn't travel *that* fast. "What are you talking about?"

Layne pointed to the mess. "Lulabelle did that and now she won't come out. We can't even get in to see if her calf is okay."

Lulabell. Hell, he should have known. At least he knew what to do with *her*. "She's protecting it. Something must have spooked her. Send Nash to the south gate to help down there and get Brody over here to ride around the whole area with you. Check for tracks, mountain lion, coyote, even burro." He started for the tarp to find a way in.

"Sure. I can do that. But who will save you from her if I go?"

He halted and looked over his shoulder to see Layne grinning, his bushy mustache twitching. "Wiseass."

The man broke into laughter.

He ignored him, walking around the tarp. He had to hand it to the heifer, she knew how to protect her young. There was no way in with the metal post holding down the end of the tarp. Pulling out his pocket knife, he poked a hole in the tarp.

He got a warning moo for his effort. Quickly, he slit the material far enough to squeeze inside. Sure enough, Lulabelle had her calf backed against the corner, standing ready to protect her.

He knew it the moment she recognized it was him. She gave a loud snort then slowly walked forward.

Usually, her affection irritated him, but he understood. She'd been afraid for her calf and in her eyes, he'd protect her. "You okay, Belle?"

She stopped in front of him, and he could see her trembling.

He wrapped his arms around her. "You're a good girl. You did good."

She pressed her head against him, and he held her

until she relaxed. At least he could do something right. "Shall we check on your little one?"

Lulabelle didn't move, so he slowly released her and gave her a reassuring pat. "Mind if I take a look?"

She looked at him with adoring brown eyes, and he grinned. "I'll take that as a yes."

He strolled over to where the calf lay. The little one was the spitting image of her mother. Crouching down, he gave the calf a pat. It was none the worse for wear. Probably didn't even know what upset its mom.

About to get up, he was pushed from behind, and he almost fell on the calf. Rolling to the side he looked up at Lulabell. "Hey. I was just checking."

Lulabelle stuck out her tongue, but he managed to get his arm in front of his face as slobber coated his sleeve. Scrambling up, he grabbed his hat and gave her another pat. "Obviously, you're feeling better. Don't worry. We're going to find out what spooked you and take care of it. You stay in here while we look."

He started back toward the split in the tarp. They really needed to get the roof back on. Was that something a tourist visiting the ranch would want to help with? Shaking his head, he opened the split as Lulabell mooed a goodbye.

"I'll be back." He ducked out. Now to find the culprit. Lulabelle was the best watch dog. Even now, the other heifers seemed clueless of any threat, but after four years with that cow, he knew she was right.

His phone vibrated and he read the text from Layne.

Found the culprit. It's a dog. He's nothing but skin and bones. Was probably abandoned. You want us to put him down?

That was probably the humane thing to do. He typed *yes*.

Another text from Brody came in. *I'm keeping her!*

He erased the word and retyped. *No. Bring her to the house.* Pocketing his phone, he started for Fury when another text came through. Stopping, he pulled the phone out again.

Then we're going to need your help.

Great. Dropping his phone back in his pocket, he stepped out of the gate. Now what did Brody get them into?

Amanda stifled her hurt with anger. But it only lasted until she got inside. Leaving her satchel on the island, she headed for the bathroom, the tears already starting. She closed the door and leaned against it, letting them fall. Crossing her arms over her chest, she squeezed. Her heart hurt. How could he think she would tell her father, especially after all she'd shared with him about her rehab? How could he think she could make love with him and not mean it? Worse was that she loved him, and he obviously wasn't worth it.

That thought stopped her pity party. The man was blind. She'd been right on the mark when she accused him of not being able to have a relationship. It really was all about him after all.

Yet even as she tried to convince herself of that, she wasn't stupid. She could see how it looked. Her father had wasted no time in seeing what he could do to prevent her from working at Rocky Road. He probably would have just gone to her company, but since he'd never paid attention to what company she worked for, he decided to go after the Dunns.

Maybe it was time to confess to Jeremiah who she was. He deserved to know, now that he was improving. Moving to the mirror, she washed and dried her face. She would explain who she was and why she was here and if Jeremiah wanted her to leave, she would. It wasn't like Tanner wanted her around anymore. Though to be fair, he'd never wanted her to begin with. What a stupid feud.

Exiting the bathroom, she walked into the kitchen to hear Isaac telling Jeremiah he looked dapper.

That the man still dressed for her was a small consolation for the moment. Preparing herself, she forced a smile and walked into the den. "Where's my handsomest client?"

Jeremiah grinned. "I'm yer ony cyent."

She chuckled despite herself. "Well, there is that."

Isaac moved away. "I'll be washing his sheets and reading." He held up his phone.

She nodded. Isaac was studying to be a nurse, so he took advantage of his down hours.

Once the man left the room, she sat across the table from Jeremiah. "How did breakfast go?"

"Ate it by mysef."

She purposefully studied his shirt. "It looks like you didn't drip anything either. Is it getting easier?"

He shrugged, both shoulders raising equally.

She started with his vocal exercises, but shortly into them she couldn't wait any longer. "Good. I'm very pleased with your recent progress. In fact, so much so that I have decided you need to know something important."

Jeremiah raised his eyebrows and both were equal, which was a definite improvement.

Tanner was going to be pissed at her, but since he already was, she had nothing to lose. "My full name is Amanda Hayden Davis. I'm Bill Hayden's daughter."

The older man grinned. "I know."

"What? How?" She sat back against the chair in shock. "Have you known since I first came?"

He shook his head. "After Dr. Navarro."

That didn't sound like something the doctor would talk about. "She told you?"

"She said she knew you fer years. Said you grew up here." He gave her a sly smile, one side lifting more than the other but on purpose this time. "That and yer face."

She wasn't sure what to make of it all. "But you didn't send me away. You didn't tell Tanner."

His gaze, which had been on her, drifted away to that gone-gaze he used to have so often. "Yer kind, dike yer father before he turned mean."

Her father had turned mean? "What about you? Did you turn mean, too?"

He didn't answer right away, but finally he moved his gaze back to her and simply nodded.

It was a lot to take in. She wanted to ask about the feud, but had promised herself if she ever needed to know, she would ask her father. "So you're okay if I stay and continue your therapies?"

"Yes."

"Even if Tanner doesn't want me to?" She leaned forward, worried Jeremiah would do whatever Tanner instructed. She really wanted to follow through and get the older man to the best he could be.

Jeremiah frowned. "What does Tanner have a stick up his ass about now?"

That was the longest sentence he'd spoken and the most correct. "Me." She interlinked her fingers and set them on the table in front of her. "It's kind of a long story. But as long as you want me to stay, I will."

Jeremiah lifted his hand and laid it over both of hers. "I want to know."

The older man's gaze was steady as he looked at her. He really did want to know. "Okay."

For the next hour, she told Jeremiah how Tanner fought her at first but listened because of how much he cared. She told Jeremiah about helping with the birthing and moving the cattle, and of course, the snake. She even told him how excited she'd been about the dude ranch concept and that Tanner was trying really hard to make it happen.

Then she explained about what her father must have

done. "I promise you, Jeremiah. I would never tell my father. This is too important for Rocky Road. It's too important to Tanner. Not that I care what he wants anymore."

The older man sat back and shook his head, causing her heart to shrink. "Mandy, my son is an idgit. Idit." He worked his jaw. "Id-i-ot."

Her relief caused her eyes to tear up.

"You dove him and he's...stubborn."

She smiled, but her throat wouldn't let any words past as she fought her tears.

"We fix this. Promise." He held up his hand as he pledged his help.

She took a steadying breath. "Thank you. Even if it can't be fixed. Knowing that you believe me and understand, means so much."

"If I were better, I'd whup his butt."

She chuckled at the sentiment. "I'm sure you would."

At the front door opening, she looked at the clock. It was still a little early for Tanner to get his father's lunch. She'd probably make herself scarce for that.

"Jeremiah! Where is he? Amanda!"

At the sound of her father's voice, she froze. What was he doing here? She rose and walked around the table. She made it to Jeremiah's side just as he moved his wheelchair to face the archway.

Her father stepped in and halted. "You!" He pointed at Jeremiah. "There will be no rezoning. I'll stop it. Are you trying to make a laughing stock of our town? What are you thinking? No, don't tell me. You're thinking only of yourself."

"Dad, this rezoning could put Four Peaks on the map. It's brilliant."

Her father's face turned red. "You don't know what you're talking about."

And there it was. What her father truly thought of her.

"Jeremiah, if you don't pull that rezoning request, I'll bury this ranch."

That was enough. "Dad, stop. Jeremiah can't talk well yet. You're taking unfair advantage."

"Then he can listen for once." Her father turned back to Jeremiah, his hands moving with every word. "You pull that damn rezoning request today. The last thing this town needs is a bunch of city folk trashing the place. It won't just destroy our town but your ranch. Is that what you want?"

She stepped forward. Did her father not see Jeremiah was getting agitated. "Dad, calm down. Jeremiah is just doing what he needs to do to keep his ranch afloat. It's not about hurting the town. They could even do Town Nights in the off season so the locals could enjoy the venue."

Her father's head jerked toward her. "I can't believe what I'm hearing. I leave you a note that only loyal children live in my house and here you are defending the Dunns? The Dunns! You're a traitor, betraying your own blood, for what? Some job?"

A long low grunt came from Jeremiah. "You asshoe."

She looked behind her to see Jeremiah trying to stand,

but his knees buckled and missing his wheelchair, he went down.

"Jeremiah!" She crouched next to him. "Are you okay?"

The sound of the front door slamming closed had her looking up just as Tanner appeared in the archway. "What the hell is going on here?" His gaze swept the room. "Dad!" He brushed past her father and crouched next to Jeremiah. "Are you okay?"

"Yes."

He slowly lifted Jeremiah onto his wheelchair. Once he had him settled, he finally looked up and saw her father.

The fury in Tanner's eyes made her breath catch.

"You! Get the hell out of our house." His gaze touched upon her for a moment before snarling. "And take your offspring with you."

She had to explain. "Tanner, everything is fine. Your dad was actually—"

"I SAID GET OUT!"

His voice was so loud, she covered her ears.

"If you're not gone in three seconds, I'll help you leave."

She'd never seen Tanner so furious. Afraid her now silent dad would end up on the wrong side of Tanner's fists, she grabbed her father's arm. "Come on, Dad. It's time for you to go."

Thankfully, as she tugged, he followed. They had just reached her father's car when Tanner came out of the house, a shotgun in his hands. "Your three seconds are up!"

Before she knew what her father was about, he shoved her in the back seat. Then jumping in, he started the car and slammed on the gas, spinning them around and down the drive faster than was smart.

After two horrendous bumps that had her hitting her head on the ceiling despite her seatbelt, her father finally slowed down to navigate the rocky drive. With the ride bearable, her upset spilled over. "What were you thinking?"

There was no answer for a long while. "I was thinking of Four Peaks."

"No, you weren't. You were pissed I was working at the Rocky Road and wanted to do whatever you could to make me stop."

He ignored her. "They want to make it a damn dude ranch."

"Well, what else can they do? You blocked them from expanding with the conservation land."

"That's important or people like your ex would have built apartments and developments there."

He had to be kidding. "Not if the Dunns were using it for ranching, which they would have eventually. Did you even ask if they wanted it first?"

Her father didn't answer, which made her suspicious. "Dad, did you ask them if they wanted to buy it?"

"They had an offer in on it, but if they bought it, they could still sell it to developers. Now everyone can use it."

Her chest tightened at what a blow that must have

been to Tanner's family. "Did you do that to be popular with the voters or to hurt the Dunns?"

She sucked in her breath when he didn't answer. He'd obviously done it for both reasons. "You doomed them then. They're too small to compete with other ranches now. It's *your* fault they have to become a dude ranch. You should be cheering. You got what you wanted."

They finally turned onto Black Spur Road and headed for town. How was she going to explain this mess to LaReina? She was supposed to be working today, and now her car with all her clothes was sitting back at Rocky Road.

"They can always expand to the east. The Harpers own that and haven't used it in years. I bet they'd sell. They would be getting up there in years now."

At her father's return to their conversation, she could tell he was attempting to mitigate his own guilt. If he expected her to agree, he was dead wrong. She'd never been so disappointed with him in her life. "They can't. They've tried, but the Harpers won't sell. And before you suggest it, the small ranch in Cave Creek owned by the Fords has all the local business for people wanting their own beef raised and slaughtered, so no, the Dunn's can't do that either."

Her father remained silent.

Good. She hoped he was thinking about his actions. All her life she'd accepted his decisions, thinking him infallible. Even when her own mother tried to turn her against her father, she'd resisted, having figured out that her mother's values were not her own. She was daddy's girl. But she wasn't anymore. Now she had the full picture, and it didn't shine a favorable light on her father.

Not only that, but he'd ruined her chance for a decent man for a change and put her in a bad place with her employer. It was time to find out why.

"Dad, why did this stupid feud start in the first place? Please don't tell me it was your grandfather's doing." The thought that her life had been screwed up by some long-lost ancestor would be too much to take.

"No, it wasn't. It was me and Jeremiah."

From the way everyone in town acted, she'd actually thought it was older than one generation, though counting her brothers, it could be considered two generations. "What happened? Did he beat you up in third grade? Did you loosen his saddle so he lost a horse race in high school?"

"Actually, we were best friends in high school."

That revelation shocked her. She wished she could see his face. Unbuckling the seatbelt, she moved to the center of the back seat so she could watch him in the rearview mirror. "You were?"

"Yes. We did everything together. All our pranks were played on other unsuspecting classmates." Her father's lips quirked up at the memories.

"So what happened?"

"I always blamed it on life, but deep down I guess I was jealous. He got the life I wanted."

That made no sense. "Jeremiah lost his son, lost his wife, had a stroke, and is running a failing cattle operation, while you are a respected state legislator with a thriving cattle business. How could you be jealous?"

He pulled the car into the driveway where three other trucks were parked. Turning off the engine, he got out.

Quickly, she scrambled out of the back seat. "Dad. How could you be jealous?" She followed him into the house, where he dropped his keys and finally turned to face her.

"At the time, in high school, we were dating twins. Jeremiah and I decided we would both ask our twin to marry us. Jeremiah's twin said yes, even though he asked her during a moonlit hayride." He snorted. "I took my twin to the nicest steak place in the county. Then we went to the carnival that was in town. In the middle of the Tunnel of Love, I popped the question."

As her father paused, she could tell the ending wasn't good.

"She said 'no'. She was going to college. I told her I would wait for her, but she still said 'no'."

For the first time in the last twenty-four hours, she felt somewhat sorry for her father. She'd never known that he had proposed to someone before her mother. "That had to have been difficult."

He shrugged and moved into the living room to stand by the Riverstone fireplace. "I was young, but I was hurt and jealous when Jeremiah asked me to be his best man. I made an excuse and was out of town that day."

She moved to the Italian leather couch and sat. "So you basically ended your friendship."

He shook his head. "It was never anything official. Jeremiah had a new wife, and though he'd invite me to dinner or events, I always turned him down. Then I met your mother, who thought I could do no wrong and could be anything I wished to be. She was exactly what I needed at the time. So when I heard that Jeremiah had made an offer on the property to the west, I complained to your mother about how he would now have a bigger ranch than we did."

"Wait, did Mom know about your past with Jeremiah?"

Her father walked across the room and stared out the slider, his hands clasped behind his back. "Not everything, but enough to consider him my greatest competition, even if he had no interest in being anyone but a cattle rancher. She's the one who suggested the conservation idea. Of course, once that went through, it was an easy step onto the Town Council and soon to the state legislature. Her dreams became mine, because mine hadn't worked. Hers I could accomplish, until she wanted me to run for congress."

She knew the rest. Her mother wanted to be the wife of a federal politician and when her father didn't want to leave the state, preferring to help his neighbors, she divorced him. "So why have you continued to be angry with the Dunns?"

He turned and faced her, but the light from outside kept his face in shadow. "There were many small incidents over the years. Our sons fighting. One of us having the best prize cattle while the other didn't, etc."

She'd heard enough to know the whole feud was stupid. She rose, unable to sit still any longer, the frustration over the origin too much to accept. "And now your sons and Jeremiah's sons have kept it going. I guess it's a good thing I married Claude instead of a Dunn." What would her father think if he knew how she felt?

She set her hands on her hips. "When is it going to stop? You saw Jeremiah. He can't walk and his speech is just starting to return. Will it stop when you're too old to walk or when your grandchildren are too old to walk? How many more people are going to get hurt? Or does stopping the dude ranch and driving the Dunns out make you the winner? Isn't the fact they're struggling enough for you?"

"Honestly Mandy, I didn't know they were struggling. I didn't even know Jeremiah was in such bad shape."

She threw her hands up. "Really? Everyone in town knows he had a stroke. What did you expect, that he had a stroke one day and picked himself up by his bootstraps and got back on his horse the next?"

Her father grimaced, maybe seeing himself in the light for the first time. "I didn't actually think about the results. It's not like I'm in the medical field."

She stared at him, her mouth open. Really? Crossing her arms, she scowled. "How many times have I told you about my patients in the last three months? How many times have I talked about the struggles people have? Dammit Dad, how could you forget what I went through!"

He stepped to her and grasped her by the shoulders. "I wanted to forget. That was the worst time in my life."

She rolled her eyes. "It was no walk in the park for me either."

He dropped his hands. "I know. I know. I...I just blocked it out. When you talk about your work, it reminds me of that time and I think of something else." He set his hand to his chest. "It hurts when I think of you like you were. I almost lost you."

"I know, but you have to accept what happened and embrace the fact that I made it through, so you can have sympathy for others. Jeremiah didn't even want to live. He has a long road to recovery. Did it make you happy to see him that way?"

"No." He shook his head vigorously. "When he fell, it reminded me of you. It reminded me of who he'd been when he was my friend. I wouldn't wish that condition on my worst enemy."

Cocking her head, she studied her father. "And is Jeremiah your worst enemy?"

"No. I am."

CHAPTER 10

TANNER STRODE back into the house. His pulsebeat sounding in his ears as the adrenaline from his anger pumped hard through his body. More than anything, he wanted to hit something, anything.

He walked down the hall and locked the shotgun back into the cabinet in his dad's office. Luckily, he'd left it unloaded, not trusting himself to stay in control. Seeing his father on the floor with Bill Hayden standing over him in *their* house had been too much. He was just glad it was his day to make dad's lunch and not Brody's. Brody could be hot headed at times, even if he did think Amanda innocent of telling her father about the dude ranch.

Obviously, she was far from innocent. It was time to end her farce. He turned toward the desk and opened the file drawer before he withdrew the file filled with his dad's paperwork. After finding the email he needed, he started the computer up. It shouldn't take long to make a complaint against Amanda Hayden Davis, the physical therapist, speech pathologist, and liar. As soon as the screen lit up, he opened a new email and typed a short message to the director of operations of Elite Home Therapies, the company who'd sent Amanda. He simply requested a new person or persons as the one he currently had had released his father's condition to others. Adding his signature, he sent it off.

The satisfaction he'd expected to feel didn't come. Getting rid of Amanda was like closing the barn door after the horses had run out. It wouldn't change the decision on the rezoning, and it wouldn't save the ranch, but at least he wouldn't have to see her and be reminded how stupid he'd been.

He started to rise when a new email came in. It was from the Town Council. He sat back down hard and forced himself to open it. It was just the appointment for an environmental specialist to come out the following Wednesday. Relieved he still had time to counter the challenge with his dad's paperwork, he rose again.

Striding down the hall, he entered the kitchen just as Isaac stepped through the archway.

"How is he?"

Issac waved his worry off. "He's fine. Just pissed he couldn't get his words out faster."

"He's not hurt?"

"No." Issac jerked his head toward the front door. "Who was that man?"

"His worst enemy. Tell Dad I'm making his lunch now.

I had to take care of a couple emails, so it'll be a few minutes late."

"Got it." The big man walked back into the den.

He didn't look forward to trying to find out from his father what Bill Hayden said. No doubt he complained about the rezoning. Now, he'd have to fill Dad in. Hopefully, the news wouldn't send him into some kind of heart failure. If it did, he had Isaac nearby to help.

Picking up the tray with his own roast beef sandwich and his father's new favorite on his low-fat diet, chicken salad, he entered the den. "Are you up for lunch, Dad?"

Isaac, who sat across the table from his father rose. "He's all yours."

Taking the chair Isaac vacated, he set the sandwiches down. "If you're not feeling well, you don't have to eat this." He set the plate and a glass of iced tea in front of his father before putting his own plate and bottle of water on the table and setting the tray aside.

"I'm fine."

As his dad picked up half his sandwich and bit into it, Tanner relaxed. Taking a bite of his roast beef sandwich, he tried to enjoy it, but his anger still brewed beneath the surface and the meat tasted like sawdust to him.

"Where'd Manda go?"

He swallowed hard. "She left with her father. She won't be coming back. I won't have you subjected to the Hayden hate again." He lifted his sandwich to take another bite.

"Bring her back."

"No. It's better this way." He bit into the meat, not tasting it at all this time.

His dad set his sandwich down and stared at him. "We need her."

"It's okay, Dad. I've asked for two other people. You'll continue your therapy."

"No."

Giving up on his sandwich, he gave his father his full attention. "She won't come back. She did what she came here to do. She discovered that we are changing to a dude ranch, told her father, and he is doing everything he can to stop us." Not to mention she'd stomped all over his heart. He kept the final thought to himself, barely.

"She didn't inform her father." Dad crossed his arms, a sure sign he was digging in his heels.

"I know you liked her, but—you knew she's a Hayden?"

"Yes." Dad gave a nod. "Knowed for weeks." He raised his chin. "She's pissed at her father. She wants the dude ranch. She wants you."

It was the most his dad had said to him since he came home from the hospital, and it was all about Amanda? That irritated him even more for some reason. "She's not some angel. I don't know what she told you, but she's not coming back."

"She doves you." Dad grimaced at his words. "Tood me."

It was as if Dad knew exactly what to say to knock him to his knees. His anger began to dissipate, exposing the pain. He grasped to hold onto it. "I'm sure she just told you that because she wanted you to believe her innocent of trying to undermine our ranch. But we will fight this."

"Don't fight her." His dad dropped his arms and sighed. "If I had a daughter, I'd want her just mike her." He shook his head. "Same as her."

He didn't know what to say to that. Dad had always railed against the Haydens, having his good friend turn on him for no reason had made it twice as hard for him. Yet now he sung Amanda Hayden's praises? How did someone do that? "But she's a Hayden."

"She's Amanda, and she doves you." His dad growled. "Uves you."

Could his dad be right? If he was, that meant... The ramifications of his own actions were too painful to think about.

"You dove her, right?"

He pushed the chair back and stood. "It doesn't matter how I feel." Even as he said the words, he knew them to be true. If Amanda did love him, even telling Dad that, it meant he'd ruined the best thing to ever happen to him. "If she really did love me, she won't anymore."

Dad took another bite of his sandwich as if their conversation was over.

He stared unseeing at the table. Always considered a fair man by his ranch hands, he questioned if he'd been fair to Amanda. Had he given her the same consideration he gave anyone, or had he expected her betrayal, so when it appeared that was the case, he simply accepted it without the facts? But how could he get to the facts?

His father finished chewing his last bite of sandwich then held up his half-empty iced tea glass. "Good sandwich." After taking a sip, he set the glass down on the table and wheeled himself over to the spot in the room where the afternoon sun hit and closed his eyes.

Thoroughly dismissed, Tanner put everything back on the tray and brought it into the kitchen. His father would sleep for a good hour.

"Take your damn water bot!"

The feeling of familiarity at his father's yell, eased his psyche for a moment. Walking back into the den, he grabbed up his water bottle. His father's eyes were closed, but he wasn't sleeping yet.

Leaving him alone, he returned to the kitchen. He tried to focus on cleaning up, but his gut was churning with indecision. Could Amanda be innocent and only Bill Hayden guilty? That was the question that kept rolling over in his head. If he could just be sure one way or the other, but the only way to do that was to go back in time.

He stilled. The cameras!

Quickly, he shut off the water and wiped his hands on the towel before striding down the hall back to the office. Brody was a hell of a lot better at the surveillance than he was, but his brother was in the barn with the stray dog. Besides, he wasn't sure he wanted his brother to see what had actually happened. Though there were no cameras in dad's den, they were in the hallway, kitchen, and family room, so they should have picked up conversations at least, if not actual visuals.

Sitting, he woke the computer up and clicked on the icon Brody had showed him. The cameras came up splitting the screen in three. Nothing was happening. Where were the recordings? Searching dropdown menus, he found them. It was listed by date. Clicking on the day, he watched as the three screens opened. First, it showed him and Brody at breakfast.

He turned the volume up to the loudest. Finding the fast forward command, he plowed through the early hours.

Where had he received the text from the Town Council? Was it inside or outside? As he watched himself leave, he had his answer. He looked ridiculously tall in the footage. It must be because of where the cameras were placed. Then he heard yelling outside, but couldn't make out the words.

The next scene showed Amanda entering. Even in the video, he could see she was about to cry. His throat closed as he waited for her to come out of the bathroom, faint noises of crying coming through the speaker. His heart constricted that he had caused that. When she emerged, she appeared fine, but the hair around her face was slightly wet.

Next, he listened as she put her father through his paces. Always upbeat and encouraging, he could hear how well the two got along. It made him doubt his own conclusions about her motivation even more. When she said she had something important to tell his father, he leaned forward. As the two spoke, his gut twisted even more. She'd been telling the truth all along.

He'd totally screwed up.

Cringing at his own words after he found his father on the floor, he turned the video off. The back of his eyes itched. He'd never given her a chance. He'd determined her guilt, refusing to listen. Her points had been well-made, but all he saw was what he expected to see—a Hayden plot.

He sat back in the chair and pressed his fingers to his closed eyes. He was a fool. Why was it that Brody could see it and his father could see it, but he'd been blind?

"Because I love her." Even as he said the words to the empty room, his heart hitched. He'd had her in his arms, in his bed, in his heart, and he didn't just lose her, he threw her away. The pain he felt in his chest was like the fear he had when he found his dad, only it was worse because it wasn't fear of loss, it *was* loss.

He pushed himself away from the desk and rose. His gut complained and bile rose in his throat. He made himself walk out of the room. He deserved whatever hurt he suffered. He would regret his actions for the rest of his life.

Knocking on the window to let Isaac know he was leaving, he grabbed his hat in the entryway, and strode out of the house to check on Brody. No matter how miserable he felt, he had to keep the ranch going until there was either no ranch to run or a thriving business for visitors. He owed it to Dad. He also owed his father an apology. He'd been right. Brody had been right, too. He had only himself to blame for being a stubborn idiot. He shook his head as he stepped into the stable and walked down the row of stalls.

"What are you shaking your head for? She's not that bad." Brody spoke from the floor of the stall he'd walked to.

"Who? Amanda?" A tiny spark of hope clicked to life in his chest.

"Amanda? No. I mean this girl." Brody set his hand on the head of a dog that was bigger than a coyote, but looked a lot skinnier and he'd seen some pretty emaciated coyotes.

The spark died as he leaned over the stall door and gave the dog as much attention as he could muster. The animal had dried blood around its snout. Its fur was matted in clumps and the exact color of the desert floor. There were prickly pear cacti needles stuck in its coat, and its front paw looked infected. "Doesn't look good from here."

Brody rose from his crouched position, blocking Tanner's view. "I called the vet. I'm bringing her in tomorrow as an emergency appointment. It was the only way to get her in before they closed for Pioneer days."

Hell, he'd forgotten that was in a couple of days. They always brought horses and rode in the parade. But an emergency visit was expensive. "Are you sure you want to spend that kind of money? What if the vet says the dog needs to be euthanized?"

"He won't." Brody shook his head. "Her breathing is fine, and she can drink and eat no problem. She's just weak from lack of food. The vet gave me instructions. I'll take care of her."

He readjusted his hat on his head. It was clear Brody was determined to keep the animal. Brody always wanted a dog, but after their first dog passed, Dad had said they had enough animals to take care of.

If it had been any other day, he would have argued the point, but right now he just didn't care enough, his gut aching as if he'd been punched. "Fine. You can also tell Dad."

Brody stiffened then looked over his shoulder at the dog. Turning back, he gave a short nod. "I will, but let me decide when and how to tell him."

Shrugging, he turned away. He should go out and see the condition of the south gate himself. It was just that it didn't seem that important.

"Hey, Tanner. Why did you think I was talking about Amanda?"

Amanda? He stopped. "What about Amanda?" He turned back to find his brother walking toward him.

"When I told you she wasn't that bad, you asked if I meant Amanda."

His gut twisted, and he winced. "I threw Amanda and her father off the property at gun point."

"What? When? What was Hayden doing here?" Brody's stance looked like he was ready to pull out his own rifle.

There was something in his posture that made Tanner feel a little better. "Bill Hayden showed up to confront Dad about the rezoning. I think Dad fell because he tried to stand. I walked in and sent them both away."

Brody clenched his fists. "Sorry I wasn't there. I would have helped you."

"Yeah, except as you suspected, Amanda didn't tell her father about the rezoning. She had nothing to do with her father's actions."

"How can you be certain? I mean, before I had my doubts, but if I came upon that, I'd want to be sure."

"I am." He paused, not able to look at his brother. "I went to the video from the cameras. She didn't have anything to do with it. I even heard her tell Dad she loved me."

"Damn." Brody's comment came out on a quiet breath.

They stood there for a few moments, neither saying anything. Knowing there was nothing Brody could say, he started for his horse.

"Wait. What are you going to do about Amanda?"

He kept walking. "Nothing." Even as he said the word aloud, the ache in his chest intensified. There was nothing he could do that would fix what he'd done.

Amanda dressed in the scrubs she wore the night before. Today was going be difficult at best. Working at Rocky Road when Tanner didn't want her there was hard enough, but knowing he thought she'd told her father all about the rezoning and him showing up would make it worse. She crossed her fingers Tanner would at least listen to her after a good night's sleep.

Not that she had much sleep. She'd cried part of the night and tossed and turned the rest of it. Her eyes still looked a little swollen, but at least Jeremiah would be happy to see her. She hadn't spoken to her father since their conversation when they got home. She didn't want to see him.

Her fury over his actions in the past had her re-evaluating so much of her growing years, questioning his motives on everything from buying her a truck for her sixteenth birthday to keeping her coma secret for as long as possible. She could probably get those answers, but part of her didn't want to know. She was far too disappointed in him as it was. He'd fallen from his pedestal and too many chips had broken off to put him back up there.

Her plan was to go into the kitchen, grab a yogurt, and stop on the side of the Rocky Road Ranch driveway and eat. If her father was still home, she'd tell him she needed to get to work early because—

Her phone rang. Grabbing it from her satchel, she looked at it. Elite Home Therapies showed as the caller. That was odd because LaReina had her own number. "Hello."

"Ms. Davis, this is Martin Reisberg from Human Resources. I'm calling to tell you that a complaint has been lodged against you. You will need to cease all services to a Jeremiah Dunn and come into our office next Tuesday to answer some questions as we investigate this."

Her breath caught. "Complaint? What kind of complaint?"

"It states here that you may have violated HIPAA regulations by telling a William Hayden about your client's medical condition. As I'm sure you know, we take this very seriously. So until our investigation is completed, you will be on unpaid leave. Do not, under any circumstances, attempt to see Mr. Jeremiah Dunn."

Her mind raced. Did Jeremiah now not believe her?

"Do you understand Ms. Davis?"

"Yes. I understand. Can you tell me who filed the complaint?"

"We will go over that when you come in. Please arrive at nine o'clock. Thank you."

As the call ended, she stood staring at her phone. Jeremiah knew how she felt. He even said he still wanted her to work for him. Of course, that was before her father stormed in, but the last thing Jeremiah had done was swear at her father. She hadn't been sure, but it seemed like when her father questioned her loyalty that Jeremiah had truly become upset. So why...

Tanner.

Even as the puzzle pieces fell into place, her fury rose. Either he was like all the other men in her life who thought her job unimportant, or, as she suspected, he knew exactly how important it was to her and lodged the complaint anyway, even without evidence! Now she was caught between a rock and a cowboy, her father and Tanner, and she had nowhere to turn.

"Bullshit." She was tired of trying so hard, at both her job and love, and getting thwarted at every turn. Stripping out of her scrubs, she opened her drawer to get her jeans. "Well, double shit." There was nothing in it because she'd packed her clothes in her suitcase and left them in her sedan, which was sitting at Rocky Road Ranch. Would Tanner have it towed? She could only hope.

In the meantime, she needed clothes. "Shit, shit, shit." Her wallet and laptop were also at Rocky Road.

Quickly, she put her scrubs back on and stalked out of her room. She found her father sitting at the dining room table drinking his coffee. She strode around to the other side of the table and scowled at him. "I hope you're happy now. Not only has my employer canceled my contract at Rocky Road, but I'm now under investigation for violating HIPAA regulations."

At his blank stare, she slapped her hand down on the table. "They forbid me from revealing any health information about my clients to others. But apparently, you now know about Jeremiah's health."

He set aside his coffee. "I'll call my lawyer."

"No! Shit Dad, not everything is about lawyers. Just give me one of your credit cards and the keys to the truck I was using."

He reached in his pocket and pulled out his wallet. "Where are you going in your work uniform if you don't have Jeremiah as a client anymore?" He held out a credit card.

She snatched it out of his hand. "I'm going to buy clothes because yesterday, someone made me get into his car to leave Rocky Road, abandoning my vehicle filled with my clothes and my satchel with my computer and wallet all at Rocky Road Ranch."

"Mandy, it was a dangerous situation." Her father's tone was soothing. "I couldn't well leave you there."

Unfortunately, his tone just irritated her. "It was dangerous because *you* showed up in the first place. *You* escalated everything."

"I was only doing what I thought best."

His pushback was the final straw. "By verbally attacking a man who can't walk and can barely speak? No, you can spin things for the people in your district, but I was there, and witnessed your driven need to tear down the Dunns. It just happened that I was caught in the crossfire, and you can't fix this. You don't even know the entire depth of what you've destroyed."

"Mandy, maybe you're just being emotional and need some time to reflect on all of this."

She gritted her teeth, stepping back to remove herself from his absolute arrogance. "No, I don't need to reflect. You need to reflect on your actions, and think about whether you still want to have any kind of relationship with your *only* daughter." Turning on her heel, she stormed out of the dining room and grabbed all three sets of keys that were hanging on the hook near the door.

"Mandy!"

She slammed the door behind her and clicked each set of keys, since they all looked alike. When the truck unlocked, she threw the other two sets on the picnic table under the porch and strode forward. She had no doubt her father wouldn't follow her because that would mean he cared about her career, about what was important to her. Plus, that meant rising from the table before his coffee was finished.

Yanking the truck door open, she got in and started it, leaving her family home as fast as she could. If she stayed any longer, she would say something that she could never take back. She wanted to yell at her father, but the person she wanted to beat on was Tanner. That he would do something so mean had her rethinking everything she knew about him. She was just glad he showed his true colors before she told him how she felt. She should have known. He was a cowboy after all.

Once off the ranch, she finally cooled down enough to determine her first stops. Unfortunately, Main Street was packed, reminding her that Pioneer Days started tomorrow.

She found a parking space behind the Lucky Lasso Saloon and Hotel, an Old West themed place that was rarely full, except during Pioneer Days. As much as she'd like a drink, it was far too early, so she walked down the boardwalk to a western clothing store and bought a few outfits. After stopping at the local pharmacy for toiletries, she headed back to the truck. She was about to walk down the side street where she parked, when she stopped.

She really didn't want to go back to her father's place. Her appointment to see the house her old classmate had set up for her wasn't for a couple more days. Basically, she had nowhere to go.

While the traffic was heavy, the boardwalk on Main Street was not. She turned back to the entrance of the hotel and walked in.

"May I help you?"

She recognized the woman from her school days. She looked the same, only prettier with a bit more weight. She'd always been as thin as a pitchfork in high school. "Hi, Ava. You wouldn't have a room, would you?"

"Mandy Hayden? I'd heard you were back in town. How are you?"

That was far too big a question to answer. "I'm good. It looks like the place is hopping."

Ava grinned. "This week anyway. Aren't you staying at your Dad's place?"

And there was the problem with a small town. "I was, but it's too much testosterone, if you know what I mean."

Ava nodded. "Boy, do I. I have three boys of my own at home. Mama watches them when I'm working, and this weekend I'll practically be living here."

Three boys already? Had life really happened that fast? "I'm just staying for a few days until I can find my own place. Do you have any rooms? I'm not picky."

Ava moved to her computer. "I just had a cancellation an hour ago." She grinned. "I don't mind as I get paid anyway when they cancel so late. Let's see. Oh, yes. You'll love this room. It's the honeymoon suite. So if you run into a honey while in town, you can take him to your suite." Ava winked at her.

She forced a smile. Just what she didn't need. "That must be big. I don't need that much."

"I'm afraid it's all I have. I can give you a friends and family discount. Just don't tell Mama."

She waved off the offer. "If it's a honeymoon suite, I'm happy to pay. I'm sure it's worth it."

As Ava pulled the old-fashioned key from the little box with HS on it, Amanda took out her dad's credit card and swiped it.

"How many nights would you like?"

"Three, I guess."

"If you need it longer, just tell me. Right now it's free until October third. Mrs. Rodriquez reserved it for her parents' fiftieth wedding anniversary. I guess they spent their wedding night there. Up the stairs and to the left. It's at the back of the building where it's quieter." Ava dropped the key in her hand.

"Thank you." She looked at the grand staircase. "Will Mrs. Rodriguez's parents be able to make it up the stairs?"

Ava laughed. "No. We installed an elevator in the back. Do you need it?"

"No. I'm fine. Thank you." She headed up the stairs with her bags. Reaching the second floor, she found the walls of the hallway were wallpapered with red roses on a pale pink background, making the place feel like it was from another century. Which was true but as the original one burned to the ground in the mid-nineteen hundreds and had been rebuilt, it wasn't as old as the décor suggested.

Walking into the room, she was happy to see it had been updated with a television, coffee station and minifridge. In the ensuite, she found a modern bathroom complete with clawfoot tub that actually looked inviting.

Stripping off her scrubs, she donned a Pioneer Day T-shirt she'd bought that fell to her knees and hung up her other purchases. Now that she had a place of operations, she had to figure out her life, as in her *entire* life.

Picking up the pen and little note pad on the end table, she climbed on top of the fluffy quilt on the king-sized four posted bed.

Wallet, computer, clothes, car. She wrote those on the top of the pad. The problem with getting those back was that there was no way she was stepping foot back on Rocky Road. Her anger toward her father for causing all the problems was nothing compared to how she felt about Tanner. She could understand him assuming the worst, but he should have at least let her explain before destroying her career. She'd given him a chance. He could have given her the same curtesy. But no. He supposedly knew what happened without even being there.

The pen started to bend under her hand and she quickly let go, shaking out her fingers. It wasn't the pen's fault Tanner was a stubborn, know-it-all, who couldn't see anything good without questioning it. She picked the pen back up.

Career. She stared at the word on the pad. If the investigation found her guilty, she could kiss her entire career goodbye. But she would fight them. She hadn't done anything wrong. Her father had figured it out on his own. Was there such a defense as "small town"? She'd make her father come with her. She added *father* next to *career*.

Home. She wasn't living under her father's roof ever again. But where should she live? If she kept her job, she could move back into Phoenix, but now that she'd been out of the city, she discovered she had missed the open desert.

Maybe it was time for a new start, far from her ex in Phoenix and her family in Four Peaks. Prescott or Flagstaff were cooler. A new job?

Sabbatical. She already had the money set aside, but now she wasn't sure what she wanted to do. It had all been so clear before arriving on Rocky Road Ranch.

And what if the investigation cleared her? It wasn't like she'd go back to care for Jeremiah. Even if they invited her, there wasn't enough money to entice her after what Tanner had done.

How could she have been so wrong? Why did he seem so good? And why did he make her feel valuable only to devalue everything she was? The words on the pad started to blur and she set it aside, lying back on the plump pillows. She was not going to cry about him anymore. He wasn't worth it. He'd hurt her in the worst way, by not believing her even after knowing more about her than most people did.

The buzz of her phone startled her. She picked it up from the end table where she'd left it, wiping the tears from her face with her other hand. "Hello?"

"Manda, have you gone loco?" LaReina's voice came loudly through the phone.

She sniffed before answering. "I must be to have let you talk me into working at the Rocky Road."

"Chica, what's wrong. Are you crying?"

"Maybe." She hiccupped. "Yes."

"Oh dear. Tell me everything."

And she did...everything, even that she'd slept with Tanner. When she was finished blubbering and talking, she grabbed a tissue and blew her nose.

"Feel better?" LaReina's voice remained sympathetic as it had the whole time she spoke.

"No. But thank you for listening."

"That's what mentors are for. I'm going to HR and getting to the bottom of this. Don't look for another job. From what you told me, this is just a misunderstanding. I think I can get this fixed." The woman paused. "But I can't help with your heart."

She nodded even though LaReina couldn't see her. "I know. I think I just need time to get over him and move on." She sniffed. That was much easier said than done.

"Okay. You stay there and don't quit on me or you'll look guilty. Remember, you have a sabbatical to look forward to."

"Right. Thanks. Let me know what you find out."

"I will." La Reina sighed. "Now get some rest, watch a movie, and have some ice cream. What is that weird flavor you like so much?"

"You mean Cake Batter ice cream?"

"Yes, that's the one. Have some of that. It will help you feel better."

"Right. Thanks." She ended the call and laid back. Talking about it with LaReina did help. Her brain understood that she needed to forget Tanner after what he did, but her heart didn't want to. It felt like a shattered piece of pottery with various sized pieces scattered about, some missing under furniture, never to be seen again.

Maybe her boss was right. Maybe she should just vegetate all day in front of the television and not think about anything.

At a knock on her door, she rose. "Who is it?"

"It's Ava. You have a delivery."

She opened the door to find Ava holding a bag.

"Here you go. They said to get it to you right away."

She took the plain white bag. "Thank you." Ignoring the obvious curiosity of the hotel owner, she closed the door.

Even before she set the bag on the little table for two, she could feel the cold temperature. "You didn't." Opening it, she pulled out a pint of the local ice cream shoppe's Cake Batter ice cream. She smiled. LaReina had already ordered it, probably on her laptop while they were talking. Curious that there was another container, she pulled it out and this time she chuckled. Teddy Bear Comfort ice cream? If ever she needed that, it was now. She definitely had to try that one first.

She managed, though it was difficult, to do exactly as LaReina had suggested. She watched movies, only comedies, most of the day. She found the small gym in the hotel and hit the treadmill, something she hadn't done in months. Back in her room, she took a hot bubble bath. But after getting out of the tub, she found her mind wandering. What she needed was her laptop. The next best thing was the computer center next to the workout room. It had two computers, both of which had no one at them. That wasn't surprising since everyone was getting into the spirit of Pioneer Days, the Old West come to life.

After spending a couple of hours on one, she returned to her room with a new list. The list was filled with potential jobs. The one that she was interested in the most was a company that provided traveling nurses, but they had two openings for Physical Therapists. From their website, it looked like they placed people all over the world. That was right up her alley. Ordering room service for dinner, she then cracked open the Cake Batter ice cream before falling asleep in the middle of a movie.

When she woke, since she'd failed to close the lacy rose curtains the night before, there was just the beginnings of light filtering through the windows. The television was still on, showing a modern-day western movie. A cowboy walked onto the screen and her heart hiccupped. The hair, hat, and shoulders looked just like Tanner from behind. When the camera focused on the actor, it wasn't even close. The man didn't have the straight nose or dark brows that Tanner had, and the jawline was far weaker. Searching in the quilt for the remote, she quickly turned off the television. That was the last thing she needed to see.

As she threw back the covers, the pad with the job possibilities went flying. Padding over to it, she picked it up and set it on the end table. It was time to move forward, not look back. It was also time to be among people again. Quickly, she showered and dressed in one of her new outfits, quite pleased with how the black fringed sleeves looked on her new red shirt. The black jeans fit perfectly. She particularly liked the rhinestone swirls that ran down the seams on the outside of the legs. Pulling the new red hat from the closet shelf, she checked herself out in the mirror.

"Well, don't you look the part today." She grinned, feeling a bit like her old self. Nothing like Pioneer Days to distract her from her woes. Sticking her dad's credit card in her back pocket, she grabbed up the key to the room and headed for the door. Today, she would close the door on the past and live in the present. Tomorrow was soon enough to tackle the future. That, and of course, her exhibition ride for the barrel races.

Just as she reached for the doorknob, her phone rang. She couldn't think of anyone she wanted to talk to, but it could be the organizers of the barrel racing. Pulling it out of her back pocket, she read the name before swallowing hard and answering. "Good morning, LaReina."

"Hey, I know it's your big weekend up there, but I needed to tell you what happened with the complaint."

Gridding herself for the worst, she took a deep breath. "What happened?"

"It was dropped."

"Huh?" The answer was so unexpected, she moved to the bed and sat. "That doesn't make sense."

LaReina chuckled. "You think that doesn't make sense, listen to the rest. Not only was the complaint withdrawn, but they praised you from here to Tucson. I read the reply. They said it was just small-town nosiness and not you who had revealed your client's condition, and they were sorry they jumped to conclusions. They also said you had performed miracles with the client, and they couldn't wait to have you return."

Something wasn't right? Had Jeremiah wheeled himself into his office? Did he have Brody try to undo what Tanner had done? She had a hard time believing Tanner had a change of heart.

"Amanda? You still there?"

"Yes, I'm here. I don't know what to say."

This time LaReina laughed, clearly thrilled. "Say it's great and get your butt over there first thing Monday morning."

Go back to Rocky Road with Tanner believing she betrayed him? Not a chance in... "I need to process this. Give me a couple days, okay?"

"Okay. Maybe he realized he was an ass."

She shook her head. "Have you ever met a man who firmly believed one thing and then suddenly changed his mind?"

"No. I guess not. Okay, take a couple days. I'll stall on this end."

"Thanks." After she ended the call, she didn't move.

She wanted it to be that Tanner changed his mind, but no one who stood in their yard holding a shotgun changed their mind that quickly. Finally, she rose and returned her phone to her pocket. She had been pretty hungry, but now, the only thing she could imagine getting down was coffee.

She opened the door to the hall and strode toward the grand stairs. Walking into the lobby, she found Ava at the front desk again. She forced a smile. "Good morning, Ava."

The woman waved her over. "You had another delivery." She pointed out the large window of the lobby.

Parked outside was her sedan. Her heart leapt. "When was it delivered?"

"I don't know. It was there when I came in this morning. There's a note on it, and I found the keys here behind the desk." Ava held up her keys.

She took her car keys then walked closer to the window. A sign sat in the front dash. In big blue letters were two words. *I'm sorry*. Her chest squeezed. Had Tanner brought it for her? Did he really change his mind and believe her?

"Mandy?"

At her name, she turned to find her father walking in from the dining room. "Good morning, Dad." She kept her tone neutral, not ready for another emotional day.

"Would you have breakfast with me?" He held his arm out toward the dining room.

She glanced back at the car, disappointment rifling through her. Of course. Her father probably sent someone to get her car. This was probably an apology breakfast. Fine, she would listen to what he had to say. "I will."

They walked into the crowded dining room which was appointed with pale pink drapes and round tables with white lace tablecloths. Once they were seated and had ordered coffee, she waited, not willing to distract her father from his purpose.

"Mandy, I've been thinking about what you said yesterday." He took a sip of coffee. "Actually, I've been reflecting as you suggested."

She bit down on the need to remind him that he told *her* to reflect.

"I realize that my issues with Jeremiah have fueled you and your brothers' attitudes toward the Dunn family. I used to be proud of that, but after looking back at how that has affected your life, far more than your brothers, I understand that it is not something to be proud of. It started with unwarranted jealously and spiraled. Your mother leaving me just made it worse." He took another sip of coffee.

If he was going for a pity party, she wasn't joining in.

When she didn't respond, he set his coffee down. "I will admit I don't understand what you do or what happened with your job, but I want to make it up to you. As you stated, you are a grown woman and I've not wanted to see that. You are still my little girl, my Mandy, who needed me so much in high school."

She picked up her own cup and just stared at him. She'd seen him use the same tactics with his voters. But his attempt to play on her sympathy wasn't going to work this time.

He finally pushed aside his coffee and held one hand up as if she was about to speak, which she wasn't. "I know that's in the past for both of us. I want this unfortunate event at the Dunns to be in the past as well. I'm sorry I overstepped my boundaries as your father and caused you to have problems at your place of employment. I promise not to interfere in your life ever again."

An apology from Bill Hayden was unheard of, never mind a promise like the one he was making. She had to give it to him. He did surprise her this time. He still was obviously not interested in her career, and she would probably just have to live with that. But she was in the driver's seat for a change, which made no sense since she was on the verge of possibly quitting. "I will forgive you and accept your promise on one condition."

His gaze wavered, obviously he was nervous about what she wanted. "What is the condition?"

Disappointment that she was not important enough to respond with *anything* closed her throat for a minute. But she was cognizant of who her father was and where his self-worth lay to know that the Earth would have to open up beneath him before he would make himself so vulnerable. "I want you to mend your friendship with Jeremiah Dunn."

His brows raised as he studied her.

She didn't let her gaze waver. Her dad would see the smallest flit as potential for negotiation.

Finally, he sighed. "I can see you are firm on this. Then for you, and only you, I will reach out to Jeremiah with an olive branch. But if he doesn't wish to accept it, I cannot be held accountable."

Oh no, he was squiggling out of it that way. She shook her head. "No. If he isn't interested, you pursue it until he finally accepts."

"Mandy."

"Dad." She kept her tone firm. "I won't accept anything less. Otherwise, after Pioneer Days, I'm moving out of town and I won't let you know where I am, which probably won't be Arizona."

His eyes widened and panic flashed in his gray eyes. "Yes. Yes, I'll keep trying to get Jeremiah to talk. I promise."

Surprised that she meant that much to him, she gave him a soft smile. "Then I'll forgive you."

"Thank you. You know you are all I have left of the happy times when we were a complete family."

"Dad. You have three sons. Don't go there. I'm not buying it."

"Right." He looked around. "Where is our waitress with those eggs?"

She bit down on a smile. How like her dad to be anxious to move to another topic when he wasn't in control of the conversation.

The waitress came up at that moment and placed their breakfasts on the table. After she topped off their coffee, Amanda finally relaxed and took a mouthful of fluffy eggs.

As she speared a piece of bacon and plopped it in her mouth, memories of the morning at Rocky Road when she'd had a similar breakfast with Tanner and Brody, caused her eyes to water. Fortunately, her dad didn't see, and she quickly wiped her mouth as she blinked back her tears.

"I'm hoping you'll still ride in the convertible with me in the parade this afternoon. You know how I hate to ride alone."

She cocked her head, hoping his apology was not simply to get her to be with him in the parade. "I'm sure one of my brothers would be happy to ride with you."

Her dad snorted. "Not likely. They plan on showing off their roping skills. I swear every single one of them has a two-track mind, women and horses."

She stifled a chuckle. That was her definition of a cowboy. Or it had been before Tanner. She quickly sobered and took another bite of her breakfast, the eggs now tasting like cardboard to her.

Her father looked at his watch. "I only have a few more minutes." He grinned at her. "It's a busy day for the local legislator. So what do you say? Will you ride with me?"

Suddenly, she realized what it was about her father that she never noticed. He was a big fish in a small pond, and he liked it that way. No wonder he didn't run for congress. He truly preferred having his own little kingdom. She gave him a genuine smile. "I'd be honored to ride with you."

His answering smile was equally genuine. "Excellent.

Be at the parade staging area by one this afternoon." He glanced over her shirt. "Your outfit will be perfect. Don't forget your hat."

"Of course."

He started to take out his wallet, and she set her hand over his. "I've got this. I have a Hayden credit card on me, remember?"

"I forgot. Which I shouldn't have since it's how I knew where to find you." He stood.

She stared at him in surprise. "You know how to go online and check your account?"

"Believe it or not, I even pay my bills online now. See, your old father can change with the times."

She held back a snort as he came over and kissed her on the cheek, no doubt so the customers could see them. "See you at one. Don't be late."

She nodded, but he had already turned to leave, nodding to a few people as he left.

Sighing, she looked at her eggs and pushed them away. Just live in the present for one day. She could do it.

CHAPTER 11

TANNER FINISHED his chicken salad sandwich, pleased to see his dad's appetite was back. "Would you like more?"

"No. Saving room for dinner. You promised Mrs. Barker's pork pie."

Hell, he'd forgotten that. "That's right. Brody ordered it already. We'll pick it up after the parade."

"You're going to speak to Manda, right?"

His gut tightened. "Yes. But don't be disappointed if she won't speak to me. I was an ass. It's hard to come back from that."

"You were an asshoe." Dad grimaced, still having trouble with the L sound.

"Exactly. I'm going to do my best, but I don't have a lot of hope. Would *you* forgive me?"

His father shook his head, then grinned. "Yes."

He chuckled. "Well, she is a lot nicer than you are, so maybe I have a chance."

His only answer was a snort.

The front door closed, and they both listened as the footsteps came closer. Within seconds, Brody loomed in the archway. "It's time. The horses are loaded and the men are ready."

He rose. "Tell Isaac we're leaving."

"Will do."

As his brother disappeared, he gathered the empty plates and glasses and put them on the tray. "Wish me luck?"

"Good duck." Dad scowled, obviously not happy with his word.

He laughed. "It could be worse you could have started that with the letter F."

Dad shook his head, but there was a small smile on his face. Then he turned himself around and rolled to the sunny spot in the room for his nap.

Tanner strode into the kitchen and set the plates in the sink, before heading for the entry where his brother waited impatiently.

"We're barely going to make it. If your girlfriend hadn't picked a fight, we'd already be lined up."

"Lulabell was right. She's queen."

Brody yanked open the front door. "Obviously, the heat has gotten to your brain, so I'm driving."

Before he could say anything, Brody hopped into the driver's seat.

"Fine." He took shotgun as the other two hands

climbed in the back. "Just remember, the horses don't need to think we're having an earthquake, so go slow on the drive."

"Spoilsport."

He would have preferred to drive just so he could keep his mind off his coming conversation with Amanda. Or what he hoped would be a conversation. He'd given up any hope, but the longer he was without her, the more he missed her. Even worse was the hole in his life she'd left. That it was his own fault was the hardest part to swallow, but swallow it he would if she would give him another chance.

It was his dad who suggested the parade because she wouldn't make a scene in front of people. He wasn't as sure about that, but at least with others looking on, she might actually listen.

He'd prefer it if he had more time to prepare his arguments, but his mother always said the longer people are mad, the more stubborn in their views they become, so sooner was definitely better. Had Mom figured that out dealing with Dad?

Not one to like a lot of attention, the whole parade scheme had him nervous. The plan was to ride up before the parade started. She would either be with her brothers or her dad. He'd face her as the man he was, full of faults, but in love with her nonetheless, in front of the families of those who were in the parade, so basically the whole town. They were allowed to line the staging area. His only hope was that people were so busy talking, they wouldn't notice. But would she pay him any attention?

He shook his head. He probably didn't stand a chance.

Brody took care on the drive, but once they hit Black Spur Road, he did his best to make up time. Unfortunately, the road into town was jam packed.

By the time they arrived and got the horses unloaded and in line, the coordinator gave the signal to start.

His heart sank as the line began to move.

Brody moved Chaos closer. "What are you going to do?"

"I don't know. I haven't even seen her."

"Her brothers are up ahead. I saw Luke running to catch up." Brody pointed forward.

At least he knew she was ahead with either them or her father, who would be very close to the front. But that meant she would be done with the route before him, and could disappear among the throng. "Hell, I don't even know if she's still in town."

"She is." Brody grinned. "Waylon told me his wife saw her at the Lucky Lasso restaurant this morning."

Okay, so she was probably in the parade. He breathed a relived sigh, even as they turned onto Main Street. His relief was short lived as Brody started his tricks.

Though he'd seen his little brother trick ride for years, it always made him nervous. But the kids loved it, and Brody was all about entertaining, while he preferred tipping his hat and waving.

The crowd was large and loud. Maybe the extra

tourists would put the Town Council in a good mood. He still had five days before the expert arrived and who knew how long before the council made a decision. He hated waiting to know his own fate. He liked to be in control. As he watched Brody stand on his horse, he wondered if maybe his sense of control was just his imagination. How much control over anything did he really have?

As Brody came back down to sit on his horse, they all came to a stop. His brother leaned over again. "And now for the handing off of the baton." He shook his head. "Never did get that. It's not like we need a baton to march down Main Street."

He was right, but it was a chance to thank the sponsors and get their names out to the people visiting. It was basically the council member who led the parade the year before, handing the baton to another council member. There would be a speech, and they'd all stand around in the hot Arizona sun until it was time to continue on down the street.

All stand around? He turned to Brody. "I'll be back."

He pulled on Fury's reigns and walked him down the side of the stopped parade. His heart pounded in his chest at what he was about to do, but if anyone was worth it, it was Amanda. As he came upon the Hayden brothers, they scowled at him, but he ignored them, swallowing hard as he realized Amanda had to be with her father in the car. People in the crowd looked expectantly at him as if he were going to be a part of the baton ceremony, but he didn't plan to be. That was at the very front of the parade.

After passing the high school band, two floats, two more groups of horses, he saw the back of the white convertible. Bill Hayden sat on the top of the back seat. Amanda sat next to him on the far side, her white-blonde hair in a ponytail that stood out against her red shirt with the black fringe. Hell. He should turn back.

And always wonder what if?

No. He wasn't letting Bill Hayden or anyone keep him from talking to Amanda. She, and only she, could make him go away. Digging deep into his gut, he brought Fury up to Bill's side of the car.

When the man saw him, he smiled.

Was that for the crowd? He leaned over. "I need to talk to Amanda."

Bill's eyes widened even as Amanda turned and saw him. At first, her eyes lit, but she quickly scowled.

Hope filled his chest. Though she was obviously furious with him, that one unguarded look gave him the determination to win her back.

Bill slid to the side of the car. "You want to talk to Amanda?"

"Yes. I need to apologize."

At that, Bill sat down in the seat, opened the door, and got out. "Go ahead. I'll watch your horse."

More than a little surprised by that, he jumped off Fury and handed the reigns to his family's rival. Bill gave a nod then turned to the now fascinated onlookers to wave.

Not about to let the opportunity go by, he quickly got

in to find Amanda had dropped down into the back seat, but her arms were crossed and she looked forward.

Closing the door behind him, he slid across the seat. Now that he was next to her, inhaling her warm vanilla scent, all of his planned speech went right out of his head. "I'm sorry Manda. I should have never doubted you. I came to know you and yet I let the feud between our families cloud my judgement. Did you get your car and my message?"

She continued to look straight ahead, but she did nod.

He took a deep breath. "I was an ass. I know that now. My father and my brother were more clearsighted than I was. I didn't give you a chance to explain, or rather, I didn't keep my judgement at bay until hearing your explanation. That wasn't fair to you, to us."

She didn't move a muscle.

"I tried to fix everything with your employer. I told them it was a misunderstanding and that we think you're wonderful. I *know* you're wonderful. If I need to go to their office and tell them how skilled you are in person, I will. I'm sorry. Can you forgive me?"

For the longest time she remained absolutely still.

His heart beat hard in his chest, the need for her forgiveness as strong as the need he'd had for his father to live when he found him unconscious.

Finally, her arms loosened, but she didn't look at him. "Since you recognize what a jerk you were, you're forgiven."

Though his gut eased, the tightness in his chest remained. "Please, look at me."

Her head didn't turn.

"I love you, Manda. More than I understood. I think that's why I felt so betrayed without even knowing that was why."

She faced him and her blue gaze softened, but she remained silent.

His heartbeat started to race at her look. "And if you're willing to have me, faults and all, this judgmental ass doesn't want to go another day without you. In fact, I want you in my life for always. Will you marry me?"

Her eyes widened before filling with tears as her lips lifted into a smile and she nodded. "Yes."

Relief, happiness, and anticipation filled him, closing his throat.

She looped her arms around him and spoke into his ear. "I love you, too."

He hugged her hard as his heart filled with light. His own eyes itched at having what he truly wanted even though he'd been too blind to recognize it.

Suddenly, the vehicle began to move and they broke apart.

"Dad?" Amanda looked over his shoulder.

He turned his head to find Bill Hayden on top of Fury.

"You two ride the rest of the route. This is what our town needs to see. Not me." Even as he said it, he turned Fury around and headed back down the route.

"Come on. You heard him." Amanda pulled herself

back up onto the back of the seat. "Let's see how many people we can shock."

Not caring about the people, but happy to be by her side, he slid up next to her and wrapped his arm around her, not willing to let her go.

As she started waving, she turned her head toward him. "You need to wave to people. And smile. You're getting married soon."

He did smile at that and gave a couple of waves before leaning in. "Why is your father so accepting of me being here?"

She gave him a secret smile that promised a long explanation. "Let's just say my father has done a bit of growing over the last few days. You will even see him reaching out to your dad."

Shocked that could happen, he stared at his future wife. If anyone could do it, it would have to be her. "You're a miracle worker."

She grinned. "I know. Now wave to Mrs. Barker. She looks like she's going to faint at the sight of us."

He looked into the crowd to see the older woman staring, mouth open, eyes bulging. Smiling, he waved at her. For the next mile, he spent half the time waving at the people from town who were completely stunned and half the time gazing at his wife-to-be.

He may not have real control over much of his life, but if he had Amanda by his side, he knew he could weather anything.

Amanda turned to him. "I think we need to get reacquainted after the parade. What do you say to coming back to my room?" She pointed to the Lucky Lasso Saloon and Hotel as they passed. "I have the honeymoon suite." She wiggled her brows, reminding him of exactly why he loved her.

"I say, yes." Then, despite the large crowd, he pulled her against him and kissed her, promising her today and forever.

EPILOGUE
MONDAY AFTER PIONEER DAYS

AMANDA LOOKED from Jeremiah to Tanner. "Are you so sure Brody is going to be accepted into the Peace Officer and Standards Training?"

They both nodded, Jeremiah speaking first. "Damn kid is the smartest of us. Took after his mom."

"It's true." Tanner set his napkin on his now empty plate. "He's the one who figured out where you were staying, so I could drop your car off at the Lucky Lasso. He got online and found that Sheila Langley had bragged on social media that you were in her shop buying clothes for Pioneer Days. Then Mrs. Barker said she saw you checking in at the hotel. When Brody sets his mind to something, he figures out a way to accomplish it, even if it means going behind our backs. Like he did with the trick riding lessons and getting his small plane pilot's license."

"And the soccer team, and project manager certificate, and the fire suppression course." Jeremiah sighed.

She took another sip of iced tea and put the glass

down. "Then it sounds like he's going to become a game ranger unless you can come up with something here that you desperately need." Silence greeted her, so she popped the last bite of Tanner's homemade flatbread pizza into her mouth and chewed.

Jeremiah's eyes suddenly widened. "I got it."

"What?" She hadn't actually expected an answer. She thought they would just need time to accept Brody leaving.

The grin Jeremiah turned toward Tanner actually made her nervous.

"If Brody can get the Harpers to accept an offer, then he can be a game ranger."

She looked to Tanner who frowned. "We already know they won't sell."

Jeremiah just kept grinning.

Giving Brody an impossible task didn't seem fair. She rose from the table. "But Brody is twenty-seven. He can leave anytime, right?"

Tanner finally looked at her. "Yes, but after Mom died, Dad asked us all to promise to stay and help him with the ranch. We have taken the promise to heart. Brody could break his promise, but that's not how he was raised. Dad would have to release him from it." He turned to Jeremiah. "We have Ernesto back and with his mom doing well, he's not going anywhere. Plus we can see how these two new hands Brody found work out. It's only their first day. If being a wildlife manager is the career Brody wants, I don't think we should stand in the way. After all, we have Amanda now." He wrapped his arm around her hips as she piled empty plates on the tray.

"Yes, and I'm happy to help. Besides, you may not need that land if you become a dude ranch. I have to say I'm very excited at that prospect." She transferred Jeremiah's empty plate to the tray. "Jeremiah, you keep eating like this, your boys are going to insist you start cooking, too."

"Not happenin'."

Tanner laughed. "Dad, why do I have the feeling you're going to be completely capable of doing the things you like and not able to do the things you don't like?"

The older man shrugged, his shoulders perfectly even now. "Age has its benefits."

She picked up the tray of dirty dishes. "And that includes a nap, doesn't it?"

"Damn, right." Jeremiah wheeled back from the table, forcing Tanner to step aside as he collected the glasses.

"Whoa, Dad. What's the rush?"

Jeremiah pointed to the corner where the sun was hitting. In another week, it wouldn't even hit there, but he wouldn't need it anyway as his strength was growing daily. "I've got to get me a piece of that."

She smiled, completely happy to be among some of her favorite men. She turned away from the table and strode out and into the kitchen, Tanner right behind her. No sooner had she set down the tray then he opened the dishwasher.

She shook her head, but had learned over the last couple of days that it was worthless to argue with Tanner about the chores. So she moved around to the stools on the other side of the island and hopped up. "You know, when we get married, I'll need to take on some of the responsibility of the house. It's only fair."

He rinsed out a glass but didn't look at her. "I know. But today you're on the clock, which means no time for chores."

She gave him the side-eye. "Why do I get the feeling you're just delaying having to move Lulabell and her calf out of the birthing area?"

His mouth twitched, but he just shrugged. As he set the last dish in the dishwasher and closed it, he looked at her. "Maybe I'm delaying riding back out so I can have a little dessert."

As his gaze moved to her breasts, a thrill went through her. If only she was on sabbatical. "What happened to me being on the clock?"

He grimaced, wiping his hands on the hand towel. "You would have to remember that." He walked around the island and turned her stool so she faced him. "But your patient will be asleep soon for at least an hour."

How could she have forgotten that? They did have some time, especially since Brody had hired the two new hands to help with the ranch. She grasped him by the waist and spread her legs so he could come closer. "This working from home does have its perks."

Tanner's head lowered just as the front door opened.

"Hey Tanner, I gotta go." Brody strode into the kitchen. "Sorry to break this up." He waved his hand at them before placing both palms on the counter. "I know you don't have to be married to gift me with a niece or nephew, but it would be nice."

Her whole body warmed at the thought of having a baby. She'd always expected to, but had given up on them with Claude, who had been almost afraid of kids. "Do you like children, Brody?"

He grinned from ear to ear. "Love them. As long as they aren't mine." He straightened, slapping one hand on the counter. "You'll have to get out there, Tanner. I have to go to the vet."

She loosened her hold as Tanner stepped back. "The dog is ready to come home?"

Brody nodded while grabbing a water bottle out of the refrigerator. "Yes, but she's going to have to remain in the house for a while until she regains her strength."

Tanner stiffened. "I don't want Dad falling or tripping over her."

"Seriously, Tanner. Dad's not even walking yet. By then, she'll be in and out."

"In and out?" Tanner's brows raised.

Brody started for the entry. "Just until I get my own place. I know you and Dad aren't excited about her."

Amanda's heart melted. "Yes, they are. You just wait."

The only answer they got was the front door closing. She looked at Tanner. "I'm thinking if you want Brody on the ranch a bit longer, then you two are going to have to make an effort to like this dog. He said it's a Great Pyrenees. Those dogs are sweet and very protective. Maybe she can keep your dad company when he starts working in his office again."

"I don't know. Apparently when Brody told Dad about the dog, the only response was a grunt."

That wasn't great but it wasn't bad either. "Maybe I can help everyone get adjusted."

His shoulders finally relaxed. "You are quite good at that."

She grinned, taking the compliment for what it was worth. "Thank you. I try to be."

He moved back in front of her. "I'm speaking for myself when I say that adjusting to you living here has been easier than getting a kiss from Lulabell."

She raised her brows as she pulled him closer again. "Do I need to be jealous of that heifer?"

"Well, I wouldn't get too close to her. She has a way of sensing things and if she thinks you get more attention than she does, she'll try to eliminate the competition."

She pretended to ponder that. "I'm not sure I do get more attention than she does."

Tanner growled at her even as he titled her head up. "I'll—"

A knock at the door interrupted him, and he stepped back. "Now who the hell could that be?"

She couldn't help smiling at his frustration and was so pleased his "hell" was not for her anymore. "Are you going to answer it?"

"Fine." As he turned and walked out of the room, she enjoyed looking at his ass. It really was perfect.

"Bill?"

She tensed. Her father was here?

"Mind if I come in? I have news for you and Jeremiah."

She slid off the stool as her father walked into the kitchen. "Dad?"

"Hi, Mandy. I hope you don't mind, but I wanted to be the one to tell you all."

Tanner walked by her dad and stood next to her, looping his arm around her waist. She was quite sure he wasn't even conscious that he did so.

Her dad looked at them both and then smiled widely. "The Town Council has approved your rezoning."

"What?" She stared, her heart racing.

Tanner shook his head. "How can that be? The environmental inspector is supposed to be here Wednesday."

Her dad grinned, clearly pleased with himself. "I withdrew my complaint then showed the Town Council the report from the environmental engineer. I knew there had to be one because Jeremiah is always thorough. Some of them are not up-to-speed on these things. So I explained not only how there would be very little impact, but took my daughter's argument and sold them on how great it would be for the town."

Her eyes filled with tears as she looked at Tanner. A stream of emotions crossed his face from disbelief to relief to uncertainty. But when he held his hand out to her father, she couldn't hold them back any longer.

"Thank you, Bill. We appreciate your help. Would you like to tell my father?"

Her dad's smile faded. "I would be honored to, if he's willing to talk to me."

Tanner turned to her, and she nodded. This was worth waking up for. As Tanner walked into the den to tell his father he had a visitor, she stepped up to her dad. "Thank you." Then she wrapped her arms around him and gave him a hug, something she hadn't done since she left home for her first wedding.

He returned the hug, squeezing hard for a moment. "I may not understand your job or your choices in life, but I'm proud of the woman you've become. Don't change for me or anyone."

When he let go, she stepped back, wiping the tears from her face. "I don't think I could change if I wanted to, any more than you can."

He raised his eyebrows and opened his hands to the side. "I'm here. That's a pretty significant change in my book."

"You're right, and I'm proud of you for it."

Tanner strode back in. "Dad's awake. If you—"

"Hayden, get your arrogant ass in here."

Her father winced. "Wish me luck." Then he turned and strode through the archway.

"Luck." She spoke to his retreating back before turning to Tanner, who looked anything but happy. "What's wrong?"

"Nothing. Everything. I don't know. It's a lot of responsibility. I don't want to mess this up. It's our last chance to remain a ranch."

She walked over to him and wrapped her arms around his neck. "It *is* a lot, but the best part is you now have me to help you navigate it."

He gazed into her eyes. "I'm going to need all the help I can get."

"And you'll have it. Your father is getting stronger every day and I'm sure he'll be able to take over office operations in no time. Your brother, though anxious to leave, may stay to help until everything is ready to open. And of course, I'll be here to help in any way I can."

He wrapped his arms around her. "What about your three-month sabbatical?"

Even as she thought of all the plans she had made, she couldn't imagine leaving Tanner behind now that she had him. "I was thinking about that. If you'll go away with me for three weeks, I'll spend the rest of it helping to set up the new dude ranch."

His brows shot up. "Three weeks? I can't leave here for three weeks in the middle of all this. Maybe one week before everything really gets going."

He had a point. "Two weeks. One week as soon as my sabbatical starts and one week for our honeymoon, no matter when that is."

He cocked his head, studying her, probably gauging how determined she was. "Okay, but I get to choose where we go on one of those weeks."

She was about to say yes when she noticed the shrewd look in his eye. No doubt he'd want to stay right on the ranch. "As long as it's not anywhere in or around Four Peaks, you have a deal."

His disappointment showed, but he quickly recovered. "Good. I always wanted to see Alaska."

She widened her eyes. "I did not expect that. And I've always wanted to relax on a beach in the Caribbean. Do we have a deal?"

He smiled, pulling her closer. "We have a deal, soon-to-be Mrs. Dunn."

"Grandchildren!" The shout from Jeremiah made it clear he'd been listening and pure joy bubbled up inside her as Tanner chuckled.

"I second that."

At her father's agreement, Tanner turned his head toward the archway. "Working on it now, Dad!"

"Well damn." Surprised, she just stared.

Tanner quickly turned back to look at her. "What is it?"

Her eyes filled with tears of joy. "Jeremiah made the L sound."

His lips quickly lifted as he recognized his dad's accomplishment. "I can make the L sound too. I love you, Manda."

A shiver of happiness whispered through her just before his lips took command of hers. If she had to choose between a rock and a cowboy, she'd choose her cowboy every time, as long as the cowboy was Tanner Dunn. But even as the thought filled her head, it drifted away and nothing but love filled her.

ABOUT THE AUTHOR

Lexi Post is a New York Times and USA Today bestselling author of romance inspired by the classics. She spent years in higher education taking and teaching courses about the classical literature she loved. From Edgar Allan Poe's short story "The Masque of the Red Death" to Tolstoy's *War and Peace*, she's read, studied, and taught wonderful classics.

But Lexi's first love is romance novels, so she married her two first loves, romance and the classics. Whether it's sizzling cowboys, dashing dukes, hot immortals, or hunks from out of this world, Lexi provides a sensuous experience with a "whole lotta story."

Lexi is living her own happily ever after with her husband and her two cats in Florida. She makes her own ice cream every weekend, loves bright colors, and you'll never see her without a hat.

Visit her Website
Lexi Post Updates
Email Lexi

Milton Keynes UK
Ingram Content Group UK Ltd.
UKHW050808220624
444380UK00008B/243